Gilbert: Thanx —
best interview yet.

How Goes the Battle?

Alan Arthur

By Alan Arthur

Illustrations by Jason Berryman

D1176159

Published By
Wilson Freelance
1039 - 73 St.
Edmonton, Alberta,
Canada T6K 3K7

Email - mail to:wilfree@compusmart.ab.ca
Web site: http://www.compusmart.ab.ca/wilfree/index.html
Phone: 1-403-463-2751   Fax: 1-403-463-2751

Printed in Canada
By Parkland ColorPress Ltd.

*Publisher's note: This work is a work of fiction.
Although some actual place names do appear,
and some characters may resemble actual people,
living or deceased, any resemblance's are purely
coincidental, and there is no ill intent by the
author, or the publisher.*

ISBN 0-968-3020-2-5

For
The Thief

Respectfully submitted,
In hopes of creating smileage.

CONTENTS

Introduction

Billy and Bobby are walking along the Battle, on opposite sides. Billy sees something that catches his attention, so he calls over, "Hey, Bobby! Come on over to the other side!"

Bobby calls back. "I'm already on the other side!"

Since the publication of <u>Battle On!</u>, many people on or about the place have given me information, or shared their stories of this wandering river. Surprise, surprise. I am not alone. I thought I might be the only person who had developed such attachment to the humdrum river. Fortunately, (or, unfortunately) there are others, and collectively, we are beginning to confess to it. I suggest we form the Battle River Fan Club, but have no meetings. That way we can all be President. Meetings are evil, and lead to egoism, and absurd stratification of society.

It turns out that my neighbour is a biologist, and was involved in a field study entitled <u>Multi-Media Monitoring of Trace Metals and Pesticides in the Battle River 1989 - 1990</u>. In layman's terms, this was a pollution study. In farmer's terms it was a dirt study. When I first moved to this location, I naively asked one of his sons what Dad did for a living, assuming the child might know.

The boy's answer was a weak and conjectured one. "He takes samples."

Of course, at the time, I had no clue what specifically that meant. I suspect that neither did the young fellow know, much, for when I asked, "What kind of samples?" I got that wonderful totally confused shrug all kids have. 'Samples' conjured up an assorted variety of things, such as food, medical, blood, forensic, and the like. I was inwardly hoping he was a forensic guy, and he would be able to share stories of cutting up corpses, and the sordid like, to keep my teenagers entertained. Canada is a boring place. However, to my mild disappointment, by getting to know John, I realised he was a water biologist. Only after I did the neighbourly thing of giving him a copy of the book did I find out he knew more of the Battle than I do, to be sure. It was interesting, comparing the two points of view, that of a scientist vs. a would-be writer. Kind of fact versus fiction.

The scientific study was quite extensive and included water, sediment, plants, and animals, both invertebrates and fish. John explained that the reason we know so little about the river is because of a lack of money. The government does not see much value in studying such things as fish movement in the Battle. (Not that they should.)

Here are some quirky facts from the study, or from conversations with John or others, which I have discovered.

1) The Battle is the only river of such large drainage area in Alberta that does not begin in the mountains with a kick-start from a glacier. There is no glacier melt-water. Instead, it relies entirely on local runoff. And much of that runoff runs through cow pastures. (Fortunately for the swimmers downstream, sh__ settles.)

2) It travels some 1100 km, and is reputedly the longest river by water flow (those countless switchbacks!) in the west that flows into the Hudson Bay. I wouldn't want to be the cartographer.

3) Its drainage basin is 30 000 square kilometres.

4) Several lakes supply it, or are on it. These include Battle, Pigeon, Coal, Samson, Dried Meat (lovely name, that... Saskatoons are abundant in the area, and it was apparently a well-known pemmican making site for the Cree), the Forestburg Reservoir, and Ribstone.

5) The water pollution actually wasn't as bad as local lore would have it. The worst build-up for minerals was arsenic, although nothing was severe. (You'd have heard!) The fish (from Forestburg Reservoir) were safe to eat. The pollution gets somewhat worse as you go downstream throughout the length of the river. Six different sites were used to collect specimens.

6) There are 42 licensed wastewater treatment facilities within the basin.

7) It has many smaller tributaries or creeks. The longest and largest is Ribstone. Many of these have been altered dramatically by draining, dredging, or straightening out.

8) The clam is extremely common. There are two species, the little white one, and the bigger one referred to in <u>Battle On!</u> The big guy's scientific name is unionidae anodonta grandis, or something like that.

9) Some 96 000 humans live within this basin.

10) The only water outflow control is on Coal Lake. Fish can only go one way on it. All other lake outlets are natural, basically unaltered. There is a fish ladder at the east end of Dried Meat Lake.

11) Different fish species have different levels of tolerance for poisons, and different oxygen or food requirements. This in part explains some inconsistencies. They can simply winterkill. The pike and goldeye must be relatively tough.

12) As rivers go, it is surely one of the slowest and shallowest going.

13) Flow varies tremendously on the season, (although pollution does not, much) and there is some flow throughout winter.

14) Battle Lake has a drainage area 20 times its surface area, which is larger than for most lakes, and in part explains some degree of continuous flow.

15) At one time there were sawmills at Ponoka, and logs were floated down from Battle and Pigeon Lake areas. The Battle in general had much higher flow before cultivation for agriculture.

Knowing all this, one would wonder if the poor beast has ever gone dry. Surely, in the thirties, if the whole country was as dry as one hears, it must have been close. The year that the highway department put in the current bridge on Highway 41 north of Wainwright is the shallowest year I can remember. You could practically jump across it. (That type of water flow would do those stupid pike in.) Most of the creeks that enter the river have gone dry, or do go dry in many years. However, the river is also spring-fed.

The other personal interest I have is of fish. It seems that they *must* come up from the North Saskatchewan or winter over, as they cannot exit or enter the Forestburg Reservoir on the downstream end. As the North Saskatchewan system is rated as polluted by government pollution guys, then one can assume that the fish in the lower areas are most likely not suitable for eating. I think they must winter over in deeper holes, mainly because it seems like one helluva long swim, but then I ain't a fish. The other thing about polluted fish to understand, is that situations such as Minimata disease in Japan arose from steady daily diets of fish, not just one or two. If I were a fish-eater, I wouldn't hesitate to dig into a Battle small walleye. Most people I met won't, or don't eat the fish from the Battle. Several people I talked to even expressed reservations about swimming in it, because of pollution. Of course, this varies on where you are. Near the source in spots it is extremely shallow and algae filled all along, and not fit for wading, let alone swimming. In Ponoka at times it's hard to tell that it even is a river.

On People

There is a certain offbeat distinct sense of pride in the people from the area, especially those close to the river. This is coined 'village mentality' or in socio-logical terms, ethnocentricity. Yet, there is aloofness and disdain, too. Folks are proud and ashamed all at once. I suspect one feels almost obliged to be proud, as you are of your profession, even if you're a lawyer, and the brunt of all those clever, yet often tasteless jokes. But then, when you look at the river, pride sort of dissipates. Well, no wonder one is ashamed. It's just not the Mississippi. Odd, that. Still, one can only admire the loyalty that you sense in the rural flow. Small communities all have similar senses of loyalty, coming from a psychological need to belong, to something, to some place, to a community. So, there are those of us that 'belong' to the Battle. (I confess to being one of them, and I'm darn proud of it, too. I just hope no Japanese tourist, or person from Niagara Falls asks me to show him 'my' river, cause he sure ain't gonna see much.)

The people I have met because of this project all have one thing in common, and it is an admirable quality. It is a sense of ruralness, of down-home friendli-ness that lies in their hearts, in contrast to much of the world. They (those rural people), I suspect, are not aware of it, as those of us who have become urbanites are. For the most part, they do not truly realise what they have, in the concept of community. For only because of the contrast itself are we made to become aware of such psychological differences.

For example, an approach to selling, for a salesperson, in the city, and in the country, must be made in two different styles, should he/she wish to be successful. The rural way is more familiar and comfortable, if you were brought up there. Simply put, it seems far more pleasant. Not that everyone resembles Red Green, but at least it is usually not difficult to obtain a friendly signal, such as a smile. In the city you never know what to expect. The friendly signal may just be the same one that used-car salesman uses to get you to fork over more dough for that clunker you really didn't want.

So thanks, folks. Most especially I thank those people from my own rural roots, the folks of Auburndale, and Autumn Leaf areas north of Wainwright. You guys and gals were truly encouraging there one day in March of 1998. The sense of community that you collectively possess is of another era completely. It's absolutely heart-warming! Frankly, I miss it!

The Teeny One, Again

The Battle is just so darn insignificant, as a river. Its appearance, down along the bank, is nearly the same, no matter where you are. If you look at a map, it would appear that it should increase in size as it approaches North Battleford. Not so. It is the almost the same dumpy little creek as it enters the North Saskatchewan, as it was several hundred kilometres back upstream. I assume this is due to evaporation.

In both provinces, there are school districts, tourist zones, and sports leagues named after it. In fact, there is even a race horse (one named Battle River Hawk) or two. There was an old school named Battleview, a district named Battle Bend, another called Battle Heights, a Battle Creek, a Battle River Hall, and of course there is Battleford. I'm confident there are several more place names that I am unaware of, and could find out, should I not be so lazy. Similarly, there are literally dozens of businesses, named Battle River something-or-other.

On Canoeing

Battle River canoeing can be characterised by three 's' words: slow, shallow, and sandbars. Perhaps four, if you count the notorious 's' word that comes from the larynx while under frustration, prefaced by the word 'oh'.

Only an idiot would go canoeing on the Battle midsummer. I am not referring to anyone in particular. I myself have done it. It is so extremely slow.

4

Paddling is difficult, as whenever you stroke at any depth, you encounter sand. It is perhaps better to turn the oar around and use it as a shove off stick, as one would in rafting. The poor canoe gets stranded on sandbars, and encounters boulders. You get out and pull, only to hit another sandbar a little further downstream. It can be frustrating, especially for those of us untrained in the art of patience.

There's nothing wrong with the scenery or the company, (usually) or the weather, but gads, that river. Shallow! Might as well put the canoe into the three-year-old's backyard pool, or sit on dry land. It will take you forever to go to the next bridge. Nope, no appointments out there. You gotta have the time. At least in most places there is little opportunity of screaming, "Man overboard!" Although, that possibility could exist, as there are a few deep holes. A lifejacket would seem unnecessary. One friend, (not an idiot) told me he travelled from Wainwright to Battleford in five *long* days.

"The switchbacks were incredible!" he explained. This guy stays in shape too, so if it were I, I think it would be five long weeks.

I would write in my diary, "And somewhere north of Cutknife, Saskatchewan, we decided to set up camp for the winter."

There are advantages to canoeing, though. The most obvious is that you can sneak. A canoe can be a silent transport mode, if the people will only shut up. Herons, deer, beaver, and even fish can be silently approached. Herons and deer are more obvious to stalk, as they are above the water. Early morning and evening are the ideal times. Sneaking only works on fish when there have been no recent rains, and you can see a fair bit into the water. Goldeye is the ideal species, because of their shape. This is the truth. You can actually see them, and for some odd reason, they don't seem to panic. Perhaps they think the canoe is just another big fish, or maybe they're too blasted busy looking sideways to look up. As with pike, goldeye do not have a reputation as super-intelligent fish. We could set up a contest entitled, "The Stupidest Fish Debate." Some public-speaking fisher-guy would undoubtedly add the common sucker to this already lowly lot.

Springtime, during high runoff, just after the ice break-up, for a few days or weeks, canoeing is an entirely different matter. The current is fast, and there are no sandbars. This is my kind of canoeing. All you have to do is steer, and allow the current to do the rest. However, it is more dangerous, as the current can be quite extreme, and there can be hidden objects or depths. The water is a dirty brown, soiled by soil, and winter's mess, including manure from many a cattle farm or feedlot. As per the government study alluded to earlier, there are no rigid controls on the Battle's basin, nor on the pollutants. A canoeist would not want to be tossed in under these conditions, as besides the filth, the water is also rather crisp at this time of year. (One day I plan to canoe it in totality from Battle Lake to North Battleford. It'll have to be in late April, or immediately after a huge mid-summer rain. Of course, this is just one of those dumb ideas that will most likely not manifest. In fact, I've been planning now for some 25 years. Anyone want to tag along? Phone me at 1- 800 - Dream On.)

Deer

Where the Battle River Valley widens, deer, both whitetail and mule, abound. The endless hilly terrain and bush provide excellent cover, and food. There are even a few guides who have set up business and attract USA hunters to the area in search of the elusive Mr. Big. Local hunters think that this is a game called 'Sucking in the Americans' but in truth entrepreneurship takes on several fine forms, and who are we to judge? (People bought the other book, to my dismay. A few years back some guys sold pet rocks.) A buck is a buck. No point bucking the idea of someone getting a buck from hunting bucks. Especially Yank bucks, since they are approaching double (triple) the value of Canuck ones.

During harsh winters, (which have been rare lately, thanks to El Nino, or global warming or just good luck), the deer will congregate near the highways, or to some place where there is easy fodder. Over two hundred have been seen (by yours truly, and others) in one spot where an old-timer was unable to get his greenfeed off, because of an early lasting snow. Perhaps the deer had some method of communicating to each other that there was a feast to be had over there. "Psst. Buddy. You leave my does alone, and you can come over to this side of the river." It seemed that this must have been the case, as the likelihood of a population of 200 being very close to one field is highly suspect. Unlike portions of some of these stories, this is the absolute truth.(Some scientist should do a study of the social behaviour of deer. The government could pay some dude 11 grand a year to discover that deer can't talk.)

Bridges

In the early days, the Battle was forded. Some shallow spot was found, which wasn't too difficult, and remembered by the pioneers. There were also several ferries set on main routes. I suspect the hills at certain points would have probably caused more difficulty to the traveller than the river itself, especially if wagons were being towed.

Bridges have come and gone. I have no idea, nor do I care how many bridges have been built on the Battle. I suspect it's well over a hundred. For a long time the standard bridge was the metal frame type, a much more attractive bridge than the newer concrete ones. Some of these metal ones are practically ancient. There are still many of them in use in more rural areas, but are slowly being replaced by the concrete ones, especially on primary highways. The early bridge builders did not foresee the intensity of the occasional springtime flood. Consequently, some bridges have been washed away. When the conditions are such that there has been heavy snowfall, and then a sudden melt, the Battle can flood its lower banks, and soak down larger portions of its valley. These years are rare, and are remembered in local yore, as the flood of 19—.

By far the most spectacular span across the Battle is the one on the CNR main line a hop, skip, and jump west of Wainwright. This bridge spans the valley, not just the river. It has been rebuilt once or twice, and actually had a 24-hour guard during wartime to protect one of Canada's main supply lines from a German or Japanese spy attack. (If this subject fascinates anyone, the Battle River Historical Society Museum in Wainwright would be my recommended resource.)

How Goes the Battle?

I know several people, one cousin in particular, who uses "How Goes the Battle?" as the standard way of saying hello. Of course, it is a reference to the 'battle of life', the daily battles of getting up, earning a living, avoiding diseases, staying out of jail, not burning the toast, and the like. Each individual carries his own battles, varying in degrees from a child's battles with learning a sound, to an adult's battle with cancer. My thesaurus listed combat, clash, conflict, strife, struggle, contention, contest, fight, and engagement, as synonyms. I recently counted the word three times in the headlines in a single issue of The Edmonton Journal.

The difference for the purposes of this silly collection is that there are no rivers (that I know of) named Combat or Clash or Strife, Contention, or Fight. Battle has been chosen instead. If rivers are symbols of life, then I would like to choose the Battle as a model for mine, for it goes slow, is methodical, has lots of twists and turns, can be exciting, but remains altogether steady at its core. It is a great provider, and has natural beauty, and wisdom, as though it's been there and done that. And it has.

Ask me, "How Goes the Battle?" I shall answer, something like this, most days, anyway. "Slow but sure, it's goin', thank you."

To those readers of the first collection, who told me, to my surprise, that you liked it: I sincerely hope you enjoy this one, too.

The Dynamite Kids Blast a Rock

"You know, Martin, what bugs me the most about farming over on eight, is some of those goldarned rocks. That quarter seems to have more than its share, that's for sure."

"Seems to me, Albert, that you're just too darned lazy. If some of those kids of yours, or some of those grandkids would just get out there, and offa their behinds, seems to me that there wouldn't be so many rocks out there."

"Ha! As if you have all the energy to go rock picking. You're about as lazy as they come. Besides, it ain't the little ones that bug me. It's the big ones," Albert explained.

"Big ones? What do you mean, big ones? How big?"

"Well, Old Man, there's one out there that's so big we can't even move it over to the fence. The kid has to drive around it every time. It's in the way. I can't wait 'til we get a tractor strong enough to move the stupid thing."

"You mean you tried chaining it?" Martin took another swig of the Pilsener, and started looking more contemplative. He had that "You haven't tried my idea yet," look on his face.

Albert recognised the look. Previous experience. He always had mixed feelings on that 'look'. "Now don't go getting any bright ideas. Better to leave the rock sit there, than for you to try anything. It is just a rock, after all."

"You know, Al, you always underestimate me. I figure about six of those beers, that I can get that rock out of the way for you." Betting six-packs over silly ideas ranked right up there in entertainment value for the pair. Albert was probably ahead 60 40. But no one kept track.

Albert stared at his friend, and scratched his chin, trying to figure out what the old fool might have in mind. He figured that Martin always had ideas, and remembered that occasionally one of them panned out. More often than not, though, they didn't. He also knew that Martin didn't have a bigger tractor, or was at all likely to go out of his way to borrow one. So after a bit more scratching of the white and grey stubble, he prodded a bit more. "Well, just what kind of scheme do you have in mind, this time? Maybe I need a bit more information before I go wagering that good beer."

Martin knew his old pal Albert too well, and figured it was his turn to win the six-pack, so wasn't about to divulge any secrets. "I ain't telling, except for this. That rock won't be there, in the same spot within a week. I can borrow your tractor, eh?"

"Sure you can have the tractor. But I gotta tell you, the last time we tried moving it with the tractor out there, it just spun and spun right into the dirt. That rock is pretty damn heavy."

"Well, how big is the rock, anyway? Maybe it *is* too big." Martin hesitated, having second thoughts. Maybe even his special secret plan wouldn't budge a rock the size of a house.

"Oh, it's not that big. We got a chain around it. The tractor just wasn't strong enough is all. About the size of a kitchen table, I suppose. Weighs a bit more than that, though." Albert chuckled to himself, figuring the beer was already his.

"Okay, I guess then the bet is on. I'll come back tomorrow, and we'll start." He reached out his hand, and they shook on it. He climbed into the old Ford, and headed out the driveway.

Albert called out, "See you tomorrow around ten in the morning."

Albert didn't think about it much more the rest of the day, other than to tell his son, and the grandkids, that his friend Martin was to be by with some silly attempt to move the big rock over on eight. He invited them to come along and watch the fun. Son Will wasn't so sure. He'd seen some of these schemes. The

9

grandchildren were eager to participate, for they too had seen many of Grampa's brilliant schemes. They had eagerly watched while Dad and Grampa had tried to pull the rock with the tractor that other time. Especially they enjoyed Grampa's swearing, under such dire circumstances. Dad's stare at his Dad for swearing in front of them was enjoyable too, but they had to delay the giggles a bit. In fact, they usually liked to see things fail rather than succeed. That way there was more swearing. *Way* more swearing.

They all started listening for Martin's car about 9:30. About ten after ten he pulled into the driveway. Albert got up off the stoop to greet him.

Martin pulled in at an angle, and held his hand out the window, his palm up to indicate, "Stop where you are." He smiled and spoke, but firm still, out at Albert, "Don't let those kids come any closer."

At this the curious kids started moseying about closer, until Will, their dad, intervened. He knew that although Martin looked silly, there would be some seriousness to it all. He turned back on the kids, and firmed up the command, "Stay on the step!" His stern look always worked. They stayed on the step.

Martin, all smiley, figured that when he divulged the secret, his pal Albert would be quite disappointed at the realisation of an upcoming loss of beer. He got out, and headed to the rear of the car. "Come look at this." He gestured at the two men to follow. He turned the trunk handle, and opened the lid, so they could peer in. Inside was a box labelled "Dynamite."

The reaction in Will was not one of amusement. Immediately he turned toward the step where three sets of eager eyes peered at them. "STAY THERE!" This time it was more like the way he spoke to the dog. *Very* definite.

Albert chuckled, "Well, now, I kinda figured that was your secret. I figured you still had some of this stuff hangin' around. But you still have to make it work, you know." Albert wasn't about to give up the six-pack so easily.

Martin closed the lid, asking, "So we can round us up a couple of shovels, and go out there, eh? It'll take a couple of hours to dig around, but I figure by about 3 o'clock, I'll have some beer to take home. You do have some beer, don't you?'

"Yep. But it's probably going to stay where it is. But I'm ready when you are."

The two old-timers got into Martin's car, and stopped at Albert's shack on the way out of the driveway.

Will turned on the kids. "Everybody back in the house. I want you all to stay around the house all day. Nobody can leave."

The kids shared the confused looks but knew that Dad would explain, when they settled down. Once inside, Billy looked up, "So what was in the trunk, Dad?"

Will shook his head, still not impressed at the two old fools. "Dynamite."

The word caused a commotion, enough to bring Mother over from the kitchen to see what the fuss was all about.

May looked at Will, begging with her eyes for an explanation.

Will explained, "Those two old dogs. Martin brought some dynamite. God knows how he got it, or if he knows what he's doing. I just hope he does. Otherwise the two of them are gonna have a real blast today. We'll have to keep the kids around the house." Then he turned to them. "If you hear a loud bang, come and get me."

Mother just shook her head back and forth. "I'm not surprised. Old goats are always up to something. Surely Martin knows what he's doing."

"Oh, probably," Will agreed, "but with those guys, you can never tell for sure."

The kids were quieter than normal in their play. It was only half a mile off to where the rock was, but they didn't dare sneak over there. The wrath of the parents, and the fear from the legend of DYNAMITE restrained them to home base. They waited patiently all morning long for some sign that something had happened.

As the family was sitting for lunch, Martin and Albert drove in the driveway. The kids waited eagerly to see what Grampa would have to say.

He stepped inside, and they hushed in anticipation of the announcement. "What's for dinner?" he asked, pretending that the events of the morning were nothing at all. "Martin and I worked up an appetite."

Mom played the game, "Stew. You kids go outside now, so that Grampa and Martin have room to sit down."

Then Grampa turned to Will, "So what did you do all morning?" The kids stepped back from the table, but hung around like the bad smell of skunk.

"Oh, I was just building that granary up some more. I got the one side almost done." Ralph played along, too.

"Oh good," Grampa continued, "I meant to help out today, but you know, I got a little tied up with this other project."

"That's okay," replied Will. "There's no hurry anyway. It'll just be darn good if you guys get rid of that rock. It's been bugging me for a long time."

Billy, who had been waiting patiently for them to tell what had happened with the dynamite, rolled his eyes. "Finally!" he thought.

"It'll be another hour or so. Martin says we have another couple of things to do. You might as well bring the kids over later, then. They can watch."

Will stared at his father. "No way. My kids aren't going over there to watch you guys kill yourselves." He looked at his wife, who obviously shared the concerns.

At this, Martin, the dynamite expert himself, interjected. "Oh, don't worry. It's not dangerous at all. All the sticks are in place underneath the rock. All we have to do is string out a bit more fuse. We can all stand back a hundred yards or so, and let her rip. That rock is going to split right down the middle, maybe worse." He looked at May. "There's no way that anyone's gonna get hurt. We did all the dangerous part this morning."

Will felt the begging glare of three sets of eyes. "Can we watch, Dad?

Please. Please. Please." He looked over at their mother, who oddly, had seemed to believe Martin when he had spoken. After another twenty seconds or so he gave in. "Oh, all right."

The kids broke into ecstatic cheering. This was the most excitement they had had in years, maybe in their whole lives.

Will spoke again."So I'll drive the tractor, and bring the chains. Mom can drive you kids over in the car. We might as well all watch the show. As long as the rock doesn't explode, and we get bits of rock splattering down on us."

"No, there's no way that will happen. I've never seen that happen before." Martin spoke as the real expert should, not letting them know that this was actually his first attempt at dynamiting a rock. "Come over in about half an hour. We'll have 'er all ready by then."

It was a long clock-watching half-hour for the kids, but Mom was excited enough herself to go watch, that getting her into the car wasn't hard. May enjoyed watching the interaction of the old pair, and the excitement of her children, much more than any stupid dynamite. She drove to where Martin's car was parked, about 100 yards away from the object of attention, but across a barbed-wire fence. She was glad the fence was there, as it would be a psychological barrier to stop the kids from venturing closer at all.

A smiling Grampa Albert met them with the current information. "She's ready. Martin just has to light the fuse, and then he's going to run back here to watch with us." It seemed that Grampa, too, was caught up in the excitement, and was quite prepared to lose the six beers. In fact, it seemed he had forgotten all about that.

They watched as Martin bent over on the ground, a few yards from the rock, and then the excitement in the air rose dramatically, as he started running towards them. He clambered over the fence, and turned to watch the weapons of mass destruction do their nasty deed on the rock-enemy.

"KABOOM!" she went. The sound was like a couple of cannons going off, only louder. Grampa yelled, "Watch out, everybody!" Then he laughed, as the kids took him seriously.

The kids put their hands up in front of their eyes, and were ready to hide behind the car, should they see any flying rock bits come in their direction.

A huge cloud of dust engulfed the rock, while kid shouts of amazement engulfed the small crowd of the eager onlookers. As soon as the dust settled, and Martin gave the signal of 'it's safe', everyone scrambled over to see the outcome close-up. It appeared that the rock had not (to the mortification of children, especially) split into many tiny pieces, but anyway, the intent had been to only crack it. A close-up look was necessary for that. The adults lagged behind. Being adults, they walked. By the time they got to the bombing site, the kid-inspection was complete.

Billy gawked up at them as they neared, and called, "It's no different than it was before."

Sure enough, the blasted rock was as intact as ever. There had been one noticeable change. It had sunk substantially lower into the ground than before. The dynamite had managed to move significant amounts of soil, but darn little granite. Will smiled at the two old-timer dynamite self-proclaimed experts. "I think if you guys did this about three or four more times, the rock would completely disappear underneath. Then maybe you could just cover it up with a mound of dirt."

Billy looked at his father; not realising it was a joke. "That would take a lot of digging, Dad. And a lot of dynamite."

Martin feigned extreme disappointment, for the audience"s benefit. "I was positive this rock would split right down the middle. Oh, well, you can 't say we didn't give it our best shot. It probably would have worked, but your Grampa Albert put his hex on the whole thing just so he'd win the bet."

"Yep, you're right, Martin. That's why I was out here all day shovelling dirt with you. But, you know, I kind of figured this is the way it would turn out." Albert chuckled, "Now I guess I get a few free beer out of you today. I don't suppose you bothered to bring any, eh? You probably figured for sure that you'd win."

"Of course that's what I figured. Don't worry. Next time I come around, I'll bring the beer."

The sad watchers, after some final inspections of the failed attempt at rock breaking, headed home. It had been fun, even if the goal hadn't been achieved. The kids hat gotten to see a real dynamite 'Kaboom' and Will and May had watched the old-timer pair's friendly rivalry and bull go on and on. Will said to May as they walked back across the field, "You know, I should have known that it was pointless to bring the tractor over. Those two didn't actually have a clue what they were doing. It was just entertainment. Old Martin probably just found some dynamite around somewhere, and couldn't think of what else to do with it, so when he heard about this rock, he came up with the brilliant idea."

May smiled, "Yes, Dear, you're probably right."

Martin and Albert arrived back at Albert's place soon enough, but Martin was still reflecting on the errors of the project. "It's too bad we couldn't have drilled right into the rock, instead of just under it. Then it might have worked."

"It doesn't matter, Martin. The fact is it was fun, and those kids sure got a bang out of it. Let's wander down to the horse tank. That's where I keep my beer." Off the two ambled. When they arrived, Albert reached into the beer corner of the tank, and pulled out two Pilseners for them to enjoy, back up at his place.

On the way back, Billy caught up to them, still buzzing from the dynamite excitement. He had forgotten Grampa's friend's name. "So, Mister, do you have any more dynamite? Isn't there something else you could do?" Billy's eyes implored, "More. More. More. Give us more." He was worse than a hungry dog begging for bacon.

Martin scratched his beard, "Well, there is one more stick left. I have to get rid of it somehow."

Billy's eyes lit up, and his ears perked up like a hound's, when the coyotes howl.

Blasted Fish

Martin settled down on the bench outside his old friend's two room shack."You know, Albert, there is something else I've always wanted to try with dynamite. I've heard about it, but never tried it. Besides, I need to get back that beer somehow."

"Well, considering this is my beer we're drinking today, even though it was you who lost the bet, I don't think there's much chance of that. Your memory is going to have to improve some. Seems you always forget to bring any beer when you come by."

"Heh, heh. That may be true, Pardner, but then again, it seems to me, that when you come by my place, you don't usually bring any beer, either. And I do recall you drinking some over there." Martin and Albert were skilled fake boasters, and forever went on about each other's weaknesses, and feigned complaints, especially so when little ears were about. It seems they were also adept at keeping one eye on the ever-hangaround watcherkids.

Billy, who was listening to the two go on, wished that they would just stop talking about beer, and get back to the important topic, dynamite. Beer was boring. But he was quick enough to know if he said anything, they would likely go on about beer even longer, just to pester him. So he bit his tongue.

"Well, I'm already down six beer. I'd like to get them back." Martin hesitated.

"Okay, you'll have to tell us about your next mighty dynamite plan then. If it goes as well as the last one just did, I might be up six more beer. Can you remember to bring Pilsener, not that crap Calgary that you like to drink? That stuff is hardly beer at all." Then he turned to Billy, "Don't you have something better to do than hang around us old guys all day, Son?"

Billy looked up at his grandfather, not quite sure about that comment. Occasionally Grampa did want the kids out of the way. But he didn't think this was one of those times, so held his ground. "Nope. I have nothing better to do."

"Well, it's pretty dull here. You're not interested in dynamite, are you? Didn't you get enough of it out there watching us try to break that rock?" Grampa looked at the boy seriously, but couldn't hold it, and broke into a wide grin, thus erasing any lingering doubts in the boy's head regarding if it was okay this time to listen. Then he turned back to Martin. "So what's the next grand scheme?"

Martin was still grinning from watching Albert tease his grandchild. "Well, it's the river. I heard that if you blast a hole, that it stuns the fish, and then all you have to do is pick them up. I think they made it illegal a while back, or something, but I'm not sure about that. It would be interesting to try down on the Battle, don't you think?"

Billy's eyes widened some more. This dynamite stuff sure was proving interesting. A lot better than just sitting around waiting for butterflies to fly by, or being told to weed Mom's stupid garden.

Grampa replied, "You know, Marty, I've heard that too. I think they do it in lakes up north. But I suppose it's worth a try down by the river. We might need some help to pick up all the fish. I don't know if you and I can move around fast enough. Do you have anybody over by your place that could help? In some places there's a lot of current. There might be thousands of fish too. We could probably use a real crew. Have to be big tough men."

Martin wasn't to be outdone. "Yeah, and then we'll need some folks to skin all the fish, too. The catchers will have to be good swimmers, cause the fish will be out in deep water over the heads of little kids. And from what I heard, it just stuns them, and they recuperate within a few minutes. A guy would have to work real fast. Maybe we'll have to go to town, and put up a poster, or something."

Albert continued the line, with one eye on Billy. "But, you know, like you said, it's illegal. The cops would be after us for sure. We'll have to do it some other way. Maybe I'll have to go ask Billy's mom if she can get a few friends together for the skinning of all those fish. We'll have to start a small fish cannery over by her place."

Martin scratched his chin some more, and took another swish of Pilsener. "Yeah, and we're gonna have to get a bunch of gunnysacks. We'll need something to put all those fish into, when they float to the top. Then we're gonna need a couple of trucks to carry all the fish from the river up here. Will would probably let us use his grain truck, if we promised to wash it out after. All those fish would leave a lousy smell, eh."

"But the cops will surely notice then," Albert added. "We'll have to get a lookout up on a hill or something to watch for the cops. Maybe Billy here could do that."

But then he'll be the first one caught, and he'll go to jail. You don't want to have your little grandson go to jail, do you?" Martin fakestared angrily at Albert, for doing such a dastardly thing as having his own grandchild participate in such illegalities, and perhaps be incarcerated for it.

Albert grinned, knowing he could stop the shared line now. "Yeah, you're right, Marty. There's no way that Billy here should have to go to jail. We might as well just forget the whole darn plan."

Billy groaned at the both of them. "That's so stupid. All that stuff. What I want to know is if you even have another stick of dynamite."

Martin looked at him, in mock disbelief. "What do you mean, Son, that you don't believe all that stuff? You sure aren't very creative. You'll never get anywhere in life if you can't *imagine* success, at least. And yes, of course I have

more dynamite. I wouldn't lie to you, would I? Neither would your Grampa."
(One last stick was *more* dynamite, not much more, but still enough to be the truth.)

"Well, I don't know about you, Mister, but Grampa never lies to us, at least when it's something important. He told me himself." Billy's loyalty was not to be questioned.

Finally Grampa was prepared to get to the point. "Well, Son, Martin and I will discuss it some more. I do want to win some more beer off him. How about if me and him plan something to do with the river? We'll have to figure out the right hole to try and all that. It might take a couple of days. But I promise you, when we go and try it, I'll invite everyone who wants to, to come along, and we'll see what happens, just like today, okay?"

"Sounds good to me, Grampa," blurted Billy, and he ran off to share the exciting news with his siblings, and Mother, not sure what exactly to tell them, as he wasn't sure how much of the stuff was true. He did know enough not to ask his Mother to start calling her friends so they could prepare a temporary fish cannery. That much was for sure.

Martin was still a tad grumpy at the lack of success at rock splitting. "So, Old Boy, how are we going to make this bet this time? I want to break even on the dynamite betting. I'm down six beer already."

Albert looked at him. "Well, last time I kind of suckered you in, I guess. I kind of figured that rock wasn't going to split, especially when you didn't put any dynamite right into it. But those Battle holes are pretty big. Each one probably has a lot of fish in it. I would imagine we should negotiate some on the number of fish we're going to get. Probably, if it works, I would think there'd be a hundred fish or so. Maybe a few less. I've seen whole schools of suckers just lying out there. Might be a whole lot of them."

Martin wasn't about to be duped by this line of bull, again. "You know, I don't believe a darn word of that. In fact, since I've never done it before, I'm going to be surprised if we even get a single fish. You said yourself that you only *heard* about this, that you haven't actually seen it."

"But what I heard about included a whole lot of fish. The guy said they filled their whole boat, and coulda filled two, if they'd had another one." If Martin wanted bull, it was bull he would get.

"But that was on a lake. This is just the river. It's a lot smaller."

"Yeah, I suppose. And there may not be any schools of suckers. Probably just jacks and walleye. The spot I have in mind looked pretty deep last time I was there. Probably has a lot of jacks in it. How about fifty? If we get more than fifty, you win." Albert had dropped his opening negotiation from 100 to 50 rather quickly.

Martin wasn't about to banter on forever, so put his final offer up front and on the table. "Look, Old Boy, I'll bet six beers that we get at least one fish. That's all. I mean, I don't even know what I'm doing with the explosive. I'm already

17

out one six-pack over this stupid dynamite. If we don't get a single fish, I'll be out two."

As before, Albert figured *this* dynamite deal wasn't going to pan out either. He figured he had a fool of a friend right where he wanted him. If only the fool could remember to bring the beer. "You're on, then. One fish it is." He stuck out his arm to shake on the negotiated bet, as always.

Meanwhile, Billy had arrived, full of enthusiasm, at the main house.

"They're gonna blast some fish, Mom!" he informed her, excitedly, as he entered the kitchen.

She turned and looked at him. "Billy, when are you going to learn that when those two get to talking, you can't believe everything they say? In fact, some days it's hard to believe anything. I was surprised today, though. They actually did try something. It wasn't all talk. It was pretty funny, don't you think?"

"Well, we still didn't get that damn rock out of the way." As he said the 'damn' his mouth gaped, for he knew exactly what was coming next. For some reason, it was okay for Grampa to use certain words but not okay for him, and whenever he hung out with Grampa, he picked up the bad lingo.

"Bill, you know you're not supposed to talk like that. You've been hanging out with those old guys too much lately. If I hear another word like that today, I'm going to have to ask you not to visit with them for a while." Billy grimaced, and wished for the moment, that these scoldings were easier for him to take. He wished he could take the scolding like a man.

"But, Mom, they're interesting."

"That they are, Son. That they are. Let me know when they actually have another plan, okay." She didn't want to admit to him that the child in her couldn't wait, either. Somehow, that was undignified, unbecoming of a woman.

"They told me that they had to organise it, to decide where they were going to do it and all that. Once they get organised, they'll let us know."

"Oh, I'm sure they will, Billy. I'm sure they will." May realised that although the two old geezers did enjoy trying these far out schemes, perhaps the attention it brought them was the more powerful motivator. There was also the delightful entertainment for the audience. The essence of the problem was that the old buggers were semi-retired but still had plenty of ideas swarming in their heads. The younger busier farm men simply didn't have the time to play around with such things.

The whole thing was put on the back burner, until further notice. Billy did see Martin's car come and go a couple of times over the next few days, and wondered what they were up to, but Grampa had promised he'd let them in on the fun, when it was ready.

Saturday night at the supper table, Grampa declared, "Tomorrow morning is the time. Martin and I are going to get us some fish. I don't suppose anyone here would be interested."

Billy, the idiot, stepped right up to the suckering. "I am, Grampa." Grampa had an unblemished record when it came to fishing for attention, or for volunteers. He always caught Billy.

"I kind of had a hankerin' that you might be, Son." Grampa smiled at the boy, and winked at Will, who was glad his father had decided on Sunday morning, as Sunday was take-a-breather day anyway. Even though they had quit going to church, the resting part, the best part, continued on."So does anyone really want to hear about the plan?"

Billy, after the 'You're an idiot for appearing so ridiculously excited,' looks from the last time, hesitated to jump right in this time around.

So Grampa pretended to give up on the idea. "Well, I guess it's not important then. You'll all find out tomorrow. That is, if anyone decides to come along. If you're still at all interested."

Billy couldn't restrain himself. "Grampa, we're interested. Can't you tell? Jeepers! Just tell us your damn plan!"

May stared at him for about five seconds, then stared at his Grampa for another five. Her message got across to both of them.

"Well, if you insist," said Grampa. "What we had in mind was the hole that's about a half-mile downstream from the bridge. Will knows the one I mean. We thought that some of the kids could walk down one side of the river, and the rest of us could go down the other side. If there are any fish, and the dynamite idea works, they'll probably float downstream, or just surface. The water is shallower downstream, and you can wade in from the west side to retrieve them. The kids would be good at that. Martin and I already scouted it out. Maybe we can have fish for lunch tomorrow, eh?"

Billy looked up admiringly, "That sure sounds like a great plan to me, Grampa. I'm coming, for sure. You can count me in."

Will paused for a moment. "You're sure Martin knows what he's doing, eh?" Will was glad the kids were to be on the opposite side of the river.

"Well, I think old Martin proved his dynamiting skills with the rock, eh? Maybe he didn't split the rock, but he didn't kill anyone either." (This, of course, the fact that everyone survived, was the most crucial aspect of the whole blasting calamity, much more significant than any real dynamite success.)

Once again, the squad waited anxiously for the arrival of Martin's car. Dad had figured out his role in the plan, which was to take his family to the river in a separate vehicle. He knew that Martin's trunk contained the dynamite, and if it were to inadvertently somehow explode, being anywhere close-by wasn't a good thing. Martin and Albert would have to go it alone, with the dynamite.

When Martin came, he picked up his dynamiting, beer-drinking crony, and departed. Will, May, and the three kids followed along about half an hour later, just in case. Just before the bridge, Will let the three kids out, who scampered off through the bushes on their way to the hole. Each had a gunnysack in tow, and swim trunks to change into, just in case they had to enter deeper water.

Optimistic thinkers they were, off to fill these sacks to the brim with the soon to be dead, fish. Then Will and May hurried across the bridge to catch up to the experts.

"Boy, those kids are sure enjoying this," remarked May. "And your dad is having a lot of fun with old Martin." She cared very little about any fish. In fact she hoped that they didn't get any, cause it would probably mean work. One or two for lunch would be fine, but not a bunch. She wouldn't know what to do with them. She didn't have a freezer, and she certainly knew nothing about smoking them. She wished the Metis fencers were around, because they'd know what to do. But of course, this was silly worry, for there were no fish yet, and there was an excellent chance there wouldn't be any in half an hour, either. She didn't know. It was all merriment, and relaxation.

By the time Will and May got to the dynamiters' haven of a hole, everything was ready. Having just one stick meant it was easier. All they planned to do was to have the explosive pushed out and underwater with a long pole they'd crafted for the purpose. The fuse ran back along the pole to the shore. There was no danger this time from any flying rocks. With luck, there would be a shower of water. The fuse was sufficiently long enough to give Martin time to scramble up the bank, to the safety beyond the ledge, where the adults could peek over.

The three youngsters on the other side had a far better view, but had been warned to stay out of the water until after the blast.

Martin lit the fuse, watched for a moment to see if it was going, and scrambled up over the bank, with the aid of Albert's outstretched arm.

Twenty seconds later there was a high pitched blast, of sorts. This one sounded lot different that the one under the rock a few days earlier. It was a lot more muffled, as the sound had to come up through the water. Eager-eyed spectators were also a lot nearer at hand this time.

"SPLASH!" The water sort of mushroomed up in a large water bulge, and then bubbled ferociously all of five seconds before rescinding back to normal. Some smaller waves like those from a motorboat, hit both shores.

The adults scrambled back down the overhanging bank, to the narrow shelf right adjacent to the water, and the kids, having changed into swimsuits behind the trees, somewhere, waded cautiously out into the current to have a closer look for the hordes of fish floating by.

Soon Billy called out eagerly, "Here's one!" He could see a foot long belly floating casually along a few metres in front of him in waist-deep water. He judged where it was headed, and got to it quickly enough. It was a scary sight. He'd never grabbed a dead fish before, and suddenly it occurred to him that this somewhat imaginary super dynamite game of fun, had some hard cold reality which wasn't quite as glorious. He had to grab a sticky yucky gooey stunned fish, and stick it in a bag. However, men must do what men must do, even when they're little boys. He had volunteered himself, and there was no way of backing down now.

With some quick manoeuvring, he opened the gunnysack in front of the fish, and used it as if it were a net, allowing the stunned creature to float right in. As the sack was porous, he held it out of the water to drain, leaving nothing left inside but fish. Then he scrambled back to the shore, all proud for having helped in such phenomenal ways. He didn't have the guts to peer inside at the horrific creature, which had become conscious a bit, and was doing some flopping about. Billy figured if he opened the gunnysack, the fish might spot him, and jump out to attack, so kept his hands tight around the gunnysack's opening.

All of the others, eyes straining at the river's surface, spent no more than ten minutes before Albert concluded, "Well, I think that's it. Looks like Billy there picked up the only fish from this hole."

"Could be, but at least it was one fish. It did prove that this dynamite thing works. And now we're even on the beer." Martin was quick to point this most essential part out. But neither really cared. If they actually cared about the beer bets the way they carried on about them, the friendship would have ended twenty years prior to this, in some ridiculous fistfight at some rough and tumble saloon.

Will called back to the young 'uns across the river one more time. "Meet us back on the bridge!"

At the bridge, Grampa Albert approached Billy, and the bagged fish. "Well, Son, let's take a look at what you have in there."

The fish was still flopping about, although less than before. Billy approached his Grampa, and handed over the precious sack, with the fish treasure inside.

"You think it's safe?" Grampa asked Billy, having noticed the little guy's cautious attitude towards the bag and its maybe-dangerous contents.

"Well, I hope so, Grampa. It hasn't been flopping so much."

Albert opened the bag, to have just a quick peek. Then he quickly closed it again, feigning surprise and fright.

Billy gawked at him. "What is it, Grandpa? What's wrong?"

"Well, that thing looked pretty *darn* mad. It had these *darn* huge red eyes, and a great big open mouth with long dangling sharp teeth. You ever heard of a *darn* dog fish, Son?" Every time he said 'darn' he glanced over at May, just to let her know he had learned his lesson from the night before.

Billy squirmed, "Well, yeah. In school, I think. Maybe."

"You ever heard of a Doberman, the meanest type of dog there is?" Albert was deadly serious. The spectators approved.

"Well, yeah, Grampa. I heard of those."

"I think what we have in here is a Doberman Dog fish, then, and from what I've heard they can bite fingers right off, and they're *darn* dangerous."

Martin was feeling left out. "Aren't those the ones with a bite like a rattlesnake's, Albert?"

Billy's head swayed, eyes spread in horror. "So what can we do with it?"

"There's only one thing to do, Son. We need to throw it back in, where it belongs. If it gets out, it could kill us all right here. One of the reasons they call this river the Battle is because of the battles the Indians used to have with these fish. I heard once that they were extinct, but I guess not."

So Grampa Albert grabbed the bag, and whipped it around like a baseball bat, and flung the poor fish, bag and all out from the bridge, and back down into the river, even before anyone else had the chance to see it. Just in case it should have jumped out. "There!" he declared. "Now we'll all be safe."

After watching it hit the water, Billy wheezed out a groan of comfort. "Ooohh. Darn good thing I didn't let it escape on the way over here, then."

"That's for sure, Billy. We all owe our lives to you." Grampa never let up.

May was just relieved she didn't have to skin the stupid thing, and cook it. It didn't matter much what it was. That night, in bed, but not yet asleep, she whispered to Will, out of curiosity. "So did he tell you what it was?"

"It was a Doberman Dogfish, Dear. My Dad never lies. You know that."

Just Checkin' the Cows

Paul, wearing denim overalls, suspenders, and all that other stereotypical garb that indicates farmerness, was up bright and early, one midsummer morn. In July, in Alberta, here by the Battle, dawn arrives about 4 o'clock. So if a farmer has the malady of restlessness, or the malady of being an early riser, he has options out here. He can go against the flow of the night owls that inhabit the earth, if he so desires. He can get out of the house, and drive or ride hither thither into the pastures that fill the gentle slopes of the Battle's glacial valley. No one would ever notice, and if they did, they probably wouldn't care.

And so it was that good Paul was up at four in the morning, out 'just to check on the cows'. A true early-morningite, this was not at all unusual for him. To a self-respecting my-way-is-the-only-way urbanite, it would be odd, but to an old neighbour farmer who knew the fellow.... "Nah. That's just Paul's way. He likes to get up." Trivial inconsequential idiosyncrasies are somehow more accepted in the rural areas. Paul, in fact, preferred that time of day, and had invented the 'checkin' on the cows' excuse, just to defend himself from anyone who may encounter him, and think him to be beyond odd, to nuts.

Four o'clock is one of the most heavenly times of day, in northern latitudes. It's not dark, for one thing. It's quiet, for another. There is a serenity that only arrives with dawn. Truly it is one of those things that must be experienced, for it is beyond description. The sun was just rising to the east, across the Battle Valley, as Paul headed south to his pasture on the north-western slopes. He stopped the truck at the brink of the hill, at a familiar spot, where he had a panoramic view of the entire valley, some two miles in each direction. Usually he would get out, walk to the edge of the promontory, and just stand there, admiring the scene, and reflecting on how fortunate he was to be there. Although Paul was a simple fellow, and not your real true deep meditation pro, still this act gave him a satisfied feeling that others could not or would not be able to share.

This morning was strange. With the turn of the key to the off position, Paul sensed it. Immediately he heard the sound, an unfamiliar sound. At first he thought it was a fool hen, a partridge, (ruffed grouse) doing its mating dance, and drumming. But after the first rift, he realised that that wasn't it. Nor was it a tractor or some other machine. With ears perked, he decided that it had to be a person, drumming, somewhere. Either that or it was one of those UFO thingamajiggers he'd heard about. "This is damn unusual," he thought to himself.

23

Paul was not positive exactly where the noise was coming from, so he got out, and moved away from the truck so he could perceive better, to figure it out. There was an echo coming from across the valley that distorted the source of the rattle a bit. He moved out to the edge of the hill, and stared across the draw, to the west. On the next hillock over, some 150 metres away, he saw what he needed to see, to explain this short-lived mystery.

There, on the hill, seemingly alone, all by himself, was a longhaired, shirtless young man, hammering away on a set of drums. The young fellow had positioned his drums so that he faced south, to overlook the valley, and seemed so absorbed in his drumming that he was oblivious to the fact he now had an audience, besides the bovines. Because of the distance and time it takes for sound to travel, what Paul saw, and what he heard, were about a second out of sync. This only added to the wonderment.

The solo concert on the banks of the Battle River Valley lasted for a few minutes, until Paul's curiousity outweighed the pure surprise of this sight. He didn't really know what to do. The situation was quite beyond the normal parameters of his life.

"What the heck is that kid doing?" he thought. He could not decide, initially, whether to just go home, and forget it, or to go over there, and find out more about this lad. Occasionally, he had had to clean up a few beer bottles out here, remnants of a small bush party, left there by some kids in town, but that was rare. He didn't think this fellow over there was having much of a party. In fact, it appeared to Paul that the young man was working, at least enough to be breaking up a sweat. For it was a cool morning and the young drummer had no shirt on. Paul did what he usually did when a decision was at hand. He reached into his left overall top pocket, pulled out his packet of Player's tobacco, with the papers tucked inside, and rolled a stiff one. As he lit up, and took that first heavy drag, the nicotine had its warming, stimulating effect. Paul, mind and body trained to the stimulant, didn't consciously notice any effect. As he leaned on the truck, and had his first morning smoke, he watched. The drumming continued uninterrupted. "Poor young man never even takes a break," thought Paul. "And that noise must be what they call rock music."

In the end, the farmer felt obliged to investigate. After all, this was *his* land. At least he could learn the adolescent's name, and pick up some details. Then when he told his friends over coffee of the odd dawn experience, they would be more likely to believe. The smoke had this way of helping him make decisions. It wasn't the smoke itself, but rather the break it gave the mind. He tossed the butt onto the ground in front of him, ground it into the grass with his boot, and climbed back into the half-ton; heart set on finding out more. Besides, maybe this kid was lonely, and could use some company.

Feeling strangely surreal, he drove the truck back from where he had come, and around the far end of the draw, to another trail, which he knew ended on the hillock where the musician was playing. His mind made up now, there were no second doubts. He was off to visit this stranger trespassing in his pasture.

Trespassing made no difference at all to Paul. He hoped the person/thing drummer guy would not think that he cared.

Out of sight from where he previously had watched the concert, he came upon a white VW Beetle. Obviously it was the drummer's car, so Paul, not wanting to frighten the guy, pulled his truck up alongside the Bug, stopped, got out, and began strolling forward towards the end of the hillock. The drumming was louder from here, as he was substantially closer.

From this angle, he would have to approach from behind the young man, who was still in his own world, unaware of the farmer, just pounding away on the drums. Paul approached with caution, not wanting to frighten, and aware that he might do just that. This was the first time he could recall having ever encountered anyone at all out here, at this time of day.

When he got about 10 metres away from the unusual happening, the drumming suddenly stopped. So did Paul. There was an eerie silence, as the remnant echoes from across the draw, and then the valley, came back. The young man put his hands on his hips, and looked up across the valley, unaware that an old overall clad farmer was just a few metres behind him. Patches of early morning fog lifted from the very bottom of the valley, a few feet directly above the Battle's wandering watercourse. Quite the sight. A vivid dreamscape from some far off galaxy, yet altogether Earthly.

Not as unusual as the sight that he was part of. The two beings contrasted delightfully. One had long hair but no beard growth, due to age, while the other had a three-day stubble. The middle-aged farmer outweighed the youthful drummer by at least 100 pounds. A strange looking man frozen in time stood behind another still, but sitting fellow, in a line, behind a set of drums. Paul the big dumb orange tabby, was ready to pounce on the unsuspecting mouse. Never in a million years, it seemed, would these two meet in another circumstance.

There was a shift in the flow, as the drummer, without seeing, perceived the other human presence. Slowly, he turned around, his thick bushy hair all flipped here and there, and became aware, now with his eyes, of the poor guy. The tension broke when he smiled, "Hi, Man. My name is Ron."

Paul echoed the introduction, "I'm Paul."

Then there was additional silence, each pondering what the heck the other was doing out here, at four in the morn.

Ron broke it, uncomfortably, "Well. Hi, Paul."

"What are you doing?" asked Paul.

"Uhhhhh... I *was* drumming," Ron answered with the tone of someone who figured the other someone would have been able to figure that out. He smiled again.

This time the smile was returned. "Yeah, I kind of figured that."

More silence. Neither of these strangers to each other was the aggressive type, in beginning any conversation, let alone one where circumstance was this unusual, or the other person was equally lacking the ability to start up.

Part of Ron wished he could get back to the drumming, and this fellow hadn't appeared.

So too, most of Paul wished he were back at home. It was becoming a race toward who could get the most uncomfortable, quickest.

This time Paul continued. "Is that your car back there?"

The question was met with an odd stare from the drummer, who hadn't moved from the stool. The silent stare allowed Paul to realise the stupidity of his question.

"If it isn't this guy's car, then who might it belong to then?" Paul asked himself, in silence.

Then he tried again. "I'm sorry. Obviously it's your car, eh?" He did what he usually did in such moments. He pulled out the familiar pack of Player's tobacco, and the papers. "Smoke?" he asked, while gesturing the pack towards the newly found acquaintance. Nicotine, that greatest of icebreakers was about to come through.

"Sure, what is it?" Ron had never been around roll-your-own tobacco, and had somehow assumed without thinking it through, that papers went with the more wacky variety, something he was somewhat more familiar with. He didn't usually smoke, for financial reasons, but this seemed like an opportunity to warm up to the fellow. Sharing anything does that.

"Player's", answered Paul, as he handed Ron the papers, and pack. "Do you know how to roll?"

"Oh, yeah." Ron grinned a grin that Paul did not understand. He took the tobacco, and rolled a rather bedraggled one, fatter in the middle, compared to Paul's, but it sufficed. Paul reached over to offer him a light. He took the first drag, and felt the intensity of the nicotine rush for the casual smoker.

Paul grew more comfortable, as always, with a smoke. "So, tell, me, Young Man, what brings you out here so early in the morning?"

"Actually I've been here since about ten last night."

Paul's eyebrows curled. "Really? Then you've been drumming about five hours?"

"Yeah, something like that, I guess. Doesn't really matter." Ron was an aloof sort, and didn't really like the questions, but didn't know how to change his immediate circumstance. He felt like he was doing an interview. He *wished* he were doing a real interview, with someone a little more important, like a rock music reviewer, somewhere, instead of this old overalled farmer.

"So do you come out here often?" Paul needed the information for later, when he could tell his friends, over coffee.

"Not to this particular place, but yeah, I do come out to the river about every second night, if it's warm."

"How come? Don't you have a home?"

"Well, actually, there are lots or reasons. No one complains out here about the noise. I like the fresh air, and I like the sound the drums make out here. It's a lot different than inside. This river valley is also very awe inspiring."

"Yeah, that's for sure." Paul took another prolonged gaze down into the valley. His companion joined in the sharing of the ever-brightening morning view.

It was Ron's turn to question. "So what brings you here?"

"Checkin' on the cows." Paul had had that reason so implanted in his mind, that it just poured out, even though this was the very first time he had ever employed it. It was his prepared defence mechanism of offering up his sanity to anyone who might question it.

Ron looked at him doubtfully, and chuckled. "You're lying. There's no reason to look at the cows at four in the morning."

The old fellow looked bedaffled by this. He hadn't met very many people who were so intuitive. Firstly, this guy had 'sensed' his presence, and now this. It was like he was a mind reader. "Well..." He paused, caught in the lie.

Ron broke the silence. "You probably just like it out here. Kind of like me. It's quiet, pretty, and all that."

Paul grinned, "Gawdamn, Kid, you know, you're right. I do just like it out here."

Ron continued advising. "There's nothing wrong in doing what you feel like doing. Lot's of people would think I'm nuts to be out here with my drums, but I don't really care what they think. Basically, no one knows, anyway, except for my mother, and she's just darn happy I have a place to play all night that doesn't keep her up."

Ron looked at his newly found friend, wishing to offer something back, for the smoke, but having nothing concrete. "Would you like to try playing the drums?" he asked.

Paul had no musical background, had no idea at all, about drums, or anything. This was the closest he had ever been to a set. "Well..." He hesitated.

"It's easy. Come on, I'll show you." Ron got up off the stool for the first time since Paul had arrived. He handed the sticks to the old farmer. "I'll teach you the first couple of beats of the song I was practising."

Paul grasped the sticks carefully, and was hesitant to sit down. "I don't want to break anything."

"Don't worry. They make those stools really strong. There's no way you can break it."

"Okay, then." Paul shook his head, not believing this experience himself. The idea that he should be out here at all, then the drummer, and now this: he was going to be the drummer. It was too much, and it overwhelmed him. He stopped short of getting on the seat. "Uhhhh, I'm not sure I want to do this." He stood back up.

"Tell you what," said Ron, "I'll play you the song, and then after you see how hard I hit the drums, you'll know that you can't wreck anything. Okay?"

Paul reached into his overalls to get another smoke while he watched Ron prepare himself with a few deep breaths and closing of eyes to focus. It was one thing to hammer away by yourself, but now he had an audience, and had more to prove. He wanted to get through the whole song flawlessly, and this was a great

27

opportunity, as obviously his audience wouldn't have a clue as to the correctness of the song.

He played away for seven minutes or so, while the audience watched on in admiration. There was a lot of quickness and memory, and Paul was impressed.

When the drum solo was over, Ron looked up. "That one's fairly easy. There are a lot of songs harder."

Paul questioned, "That's not the whole song, is it?"

"Oh, no. Of course there are other instruments. That's just the drum part."

"What's the name of the band who plays that song?" Paul was becoming mildly enthusiastic regarding this new field. For his fielded consciousness, it was a monumental step away from cows, grain, and pigs.

"The band's name is Led Zeppelin. Their most famous song is Stairway to Heaven."

"Hmmm." Paul, not one for introspection, seemed to be into a moment of such. "Kinda like over there?" He pointed across the draw to the hillside from where he had originally spotted the drummer. "You see those steps going up the hill?"

Ron stood to look. "Hey, yeah. I never noticed that before. Interesting. Jeez, Man, that does look like steps, doesn't it?"

On the hillside were natural terraces, probably made by the glaciers, on an annual basis some 10 000 years ago. Indeed they did look like steps, or a stair- way.

Paul glowed in the fact that he had done something intuitive. "You know, I think I'll skip the drumming. I think I'll stick to farming, eh? But Kid, I tell you what. You can come out here anytime you want, daytime or night-time. This is my pasture, and you're welcome to use it as a practice place, any time at all."

"Jeez, Man. That's nice of you. I do worry about trespassing and that. Cool! Now I have a place I know I can go to all the time."

"I'm gonna go home now, and fix myself some breakfast. I'm finished checkin' the cows this morning." He headed towards the truck.

"Paul?" Ron called. Can you do me another favour?"

"Sure. What?" Paul turned to face him, partly thinking that he'd gone too far, and now this damn hippy kid might ask him for something else, like hold a party here, or something.

"Can I bum another smoke?"

Twice Burned

There is a pile of truth to the saying: "You can take the boy from the country, but not the country from the boy." Many would argue it is more than a saying; rather, it is fact. Assuredly, it is a simplistic way to explain how early childhood memories may fade, but remain strong forever. Memories, pleasant, and unpleasant, run deep, affecting the human personality in so many unseen ways. In later years, we find solace in the past, in recreating situations that are fond memories of childhood. A classic example is the return to a spot where something significant happened. If a couple honeymooned in Banff or Niagara, it seems altogether fitting that an ideal anniversary gift is to have a return visit. (We fancy the spark might be hotter the second time.) It seems that as humans age, or get busied with survival, the times in which we are able to recreate those memories become further and further apart.

Herman, a schoolteacher of tremendous local fame, fished the Battle's shallow water, as a kid. He wasn't much of a fisherman, nor was his brother, Kurt, or his Dad. It was more the long hike into the isolated hole that impressed them. In later years, Herman referred to it as his 'favourite fishing hole', even though some trips ended in his being skunked, or otherwise duped, by fate, as this story relates. But such poor luck is a part of every fisherman's path in life. Only the real insecure lying braggart of a fisherman has never been skunked. Fortunately for spouses and acquaintances that do not partake in the sport, most real fishermen are able to see the humour in such failures. The ability to laugh at one's folly is a gift, especially for Canucks, it seems. Witness the popularity of television's 22 Minutes. We do have a knack for self-depreciation for both ourselves personally, and our culture collectively. If a fisherman doesn't have this skill, he's in over his head with any witty buddies. Subtle (and not so subtle) 'who's the better' verbal shots seem to instinctively accompany the sport, and its participants. If horseracing is the sport of kings, then fishing is the sport of braggarts.

To get to this hole (the Macklin hole, from Battle On!) was arduous; no matter which way you had learned. Herman's way was a long walk upstream from the south side, begun at first, by a long tramp down the hill. Other ways were by forgotten trails along the river, or by marching an equally long distance down the north side hills. Certainly, the people who were familiar with it were few and far between, and because of its remoteness, not many would go anyway, even if they did know. (Even today there are still several basically inaccessible holes along the river, secrets only to a few.) Since the fishing is inconsistent at best, no one really cares. Besides, fishing in the Battle, for locals, has a certain mediocrity, even lowness, about it. It is far more worthy of a genuine fisherman to travel 500 miles to a remote lake, and catch nothing, than it is to travel to the local stream, and catch several. Such is the foolish folly of the grass being greener on the other side.

(This trait of humanity is remarkable. One cannot help but wonder why the Japanese tourist, for example, travels to Banff at the cost of some $5000 Canuck, to see a pretty mountain, when he could take $50 and head to northern Japan, to the Olympic sites of Sapporo, or Nagano, and see roughly equivalent mountains.)

One evening in about 1974, Herman, visiting 'home', looked at his brother, "What do you say we go try our luck at that old hole on the Battle?"

"Well, it's been a long time, and I have no idea if there are any fish there still, but, yeah, I wouldn't mind," Kurt answered. "Do you feel lucky?"

"You know me, I always feel lucky," said Herman, "but I'm afraid my luck and fish aren't brothers, like you and I. My feelings probably have nothing at all to do with it. Just promise me this time that if I do catch one, you'll do your best to help me land it, and not mess up like last time."

"Last time wasn't my fault. That stupid fish dove around that log all by himself, I'm afraid. If you wouldn't have fished right beside a sunken log, he wouldn't have gotten away, like he did." Kurt remembered fondly and vividly the time he had stripped himself bare and waded right in, in a desperate attempt to help Brother land a gigantic walleye, only to have the fish get really upset, and toss the hook, thus escaping.

"We can argue all night about whose fault that was, but it certainly won't get us there any quicker, will it?"

"So let's go then." Kurt nodded in the direction of the door. In all of five minutes, they had grabbed the rods and old hooks from the basement, and were set, having time travelled back some twenty years, at a mere reminiscent suggestion.

Kurt and Herman reached the top of the valley, parked the truck, and embarked upon the trek downward. "Well, I hope this hike is worth it," smiled Kurt, who was the more avid fisherman of the pair.

"Don't worry about that. The hike is always worth it. Exercise, fresh air, the smell of silver willow. All that makes it well worth it, even if we don't catch a darn thing." Herman appreciated the rural charm more than his brother, because of it being more rare in his life now that he had relocated, and become a wretched urbanite, almost.

The brothers reminisced about their childhood trips here, as they strolled downward along the prairie. "You know, some days I miss this." Herman was so honest.

"Well, I don't know. I guess if I didn't still live here, I'd be more like you. It's tougher if I want to do these things myself. It's a lot better with company. That willow sure stinks, eh?" The silver willow along the trail was in bloom, and emitted its sharp odour.

"Yeah, I kind of like it. Weird how smells hit your memory. This stuff doesn't grow by the city. Neither do crocuses. I didn't know that, until we moved." Herman, who was in front, stopped suddenly. "Listen," he commanded.

Kurt stood still, on the plains beside his brother. "Gee, it sounds like someone else is there. That's odd. I didn't know that very many people even knew this place existed. Too bad."

"Maybe they aren't fishing. Maybe they're swimming or something." Herman remained optimistic as they crossed the last plain, to the bank, where they could observe the hole. But when they arrived in view, his optimism sank. About thirty metres beyond the bank, by the edge of the river, clearly, stood an enemy fisherman. On the other side of the river was another one.

(If anyone knows the Battle or any other small slow river, the holes are diminutive. The fish do not wander a whole lot. Therefore, once a hole has been fished at for a short spell, it gets cleaned out. This is not at all like at a lake, where the vast expanses of water allow fish to move. But at the Battle, the technique is different. Either that or you're likely out of luck. The successful fisherman does lots of moving, mostly onward to the next 'lucky' hole. Once an angler casts some twenty odd casts along a rapid line, or into a likely dark depth, if he gets no rise quickly, then it is highly unlikely that he will, unless he returns in a week or so, when some fresh fish may have relocated.)

"Well, I'll be darned," whispered Kurt, "I'm really quite surprised." The brothers descended down the three-metre bank, and sauntered across to the river. At the very least, they could find out if the enemy had had any luck, and whether or not the old girl stream still held fish.

To make matters slightly even more peculiar, one of the enemy fishermen, Jason, happened to be a former student of Herman's, and as always, with former students, and their teachers, there was a slight tinge of deja-vu, in the fateful situation. "Hi, Mr. Klinck."

"Hi there, Jason. Seems you fellows have been here awhile, and probably cleaned out the hole on us, eh?"

Jason, obviously, felt a bit of guilt, for he too, fathomed the Battle's ways. The six modest-sized pike on his stringer were probably the only ones about, and he knew it. He had mixed feelings, as did Herman. Part of him thought, "This will show you for all that homework you assigned back in grade ten, you son of a gun," although he dare not express it. The teacher-student respect thing runs deep, and remains in the psyche for an extended time, probably far too long than is healthy. The deja-vu in him could hear a darn math question coming. One that had something to do with fish or probability, or perhaps even probability and fish.

Jason, suspecting the length of Herman's trek, empathised. "Unfortunately

31

for you, you're probably right. We've been here awhile. You're welcome to give it a shot, though." Not knowing how else to politely diffuse any tension, he offered some of his catch. "And if you don't catch any, you're certainly welcome to take some of these."

"Any pickerel?" asked Kurt, who, like all fishermen who have ever read anything at all about Western Canadian fishing, or eaten them, valued pickerel over jack.

"Not today," Jason explained. "A few weeks ago we caught about ten here though. Seems there are only jack around now."

"So how long have you known about this place? I didn't know anyone else knew about it." Kurt was curious, still dumbfounded, and partly depressed, from the coincidence of someone being here.

"Since I was a kid," answered Jason, "and *I* didn't think anyone else knew either."

Although it was kind that Jason had offered some of the fish, Herman, the unlucky sportsman, had to decline. It was just bad timing, and both companies knew it. Besides, no self-respecting fisherman can accept another man's fish, for it is never the fish themselves that are the source of self-respect, it is the *fact* that you snared them, that matters. "That's okay. We'll just give it a shot ourselves. Jacks aren't what we're after, anyway, and they're not as good to eat."

Pierre, and Jason, not knowing fully how to conduct themselves, stood aside for a while, and allowed the newcomers to try their luck at the hole. But that was a waste of time. Pierre, being an extremely patient French fisherman, had stood at the hole for approximately six hours endlessly casting into the same spot. He was trying to recreate the remarkable success of a few weeks earlier, when they had caught enough walleye for a veritable feast, while Jason had wandered about a bit, and caught his few dumb pike on the other side, around, and under logs.

Half an hour of dragging in the empty hooks was quite enough. Herman conceded his bad timing and regretfully embarked upon the hike back home, chalking it up as just an act of simple cruel fate, such as having *two* flat tires on your way to pick up a hot date. (Well, not quite that cruel.)

Nightfall had approached, so Herman and Kurt, filled with the empty feeling of fisherman misfortune headed back to the vehicle. After they got outside of hearing range of the enemy, Kurt spoke, "So you knew that guy?"

"Yep. Five or six years ago, I taught him. Tonight was really odd. Two strange coincidences. Even to have some guy be there at all is odd, and then it turns out I know him. I bet you that no one else at all even knows of this place or how to get to it. I can't remember seeing any tracks the last time we came along here. Can you?" Herman was amazed at the coincidence, and being a math teacher, mentally began working out the likelihood of the event's occurrence.

"Well, at least we know that there are still fish in the river. No pickerel though," observed Kurt.

"Oh, I figure there are probably pickerel as well. Jason said that they had caught some earlier. Just not there tonight."

"So we'll just have to come back," said Kurt, although he figured at the rate that he and his brother got to this hole, it would probably be another thirteen years or so.

"Yep," agreed Herman, promising himself it would be sooner, rather than later.

But in the long run, Kurt's mental prediction was far more accurate. It's one of the noteworthy human self-delusions, to that think you will do something sooner than later. Sometimes, for some people. "Never," is a more real expectation, and all too often comes true. Fortunately for the Klinck brothers, 'never' was not the case. Just thirteen years.

It was some twelve plus one years later, then, when Herman managed to convince his brother, or perhaps Kurt happened to convince Herman, that they should reacquaint themselves with the fond childhood haunt.

"You remember that time a few years back when we went?" asked Herman.

"I remember all those trips. But do you remember?" Kurt knew that memories of childhood might vary within siblings, and never refused the opportunity to show rivalry.

"Well, anyways, I just wanted to tell you, that oddly enough, Jason, that fellow who we met down there, taught with me for a year."

"Yes, that is sort of odd," agreed Kurt. "Hopefully he won't be there this time."

"Don't think so. He doesn't live here any more." Herman knew that it was extremely unlikely for Jason to be around.

"But don't go off thinking we're going to be lucky. That should remind you. Every time I go fishing with you, you think we're going to catch millions of monstrous fish, and then something bad happens. It brings us bad luck, I think."

Herman chuckled at the silliness of his brother's insinuation. He retorted, "But I always thought it was *you* who brought the bad luck."

Kurt grinned at the thought of these accusations leading onward to deep enough sibling rivalry to spoil the trip. So he applied sarcasm. "Maybe we should just each go our separate ways. You go to one spot, and I'll go to another."

Herman laughed, "No, then I won't be able to watch you catch nothing."

"Well, here's to you, Brother. Let's have a good day," stated Kurt, as they finally climbed into Kurt's half-ton, both recognising the thirteen-year time hiatus had been too long. Kurt drove north to the beckoning Battle.

As they drove, and conversed, they tried to not talk about the unsuccessful day of the enemy fishermen, and reminisced even further back, to the more successful days prior to that inauspicious one.

But this day would be longer, for there is something that happens to a human that makes life somewhat more difficult. Simply put, we age. With that process, hills become longer, sights become fuzzier, and the days go quicker. This valley that Herman had to hike down, and the course to the hole seemed much longer than it had thirteen years back, although in reality, nothing had changed, except Herman's own perception, age-distorted.

As the brothers approached the hole, they felt that anticipation, that excitement, right before the dropping of first puck, the starting gun, or the first cast, which we all have felt. Stomachs curl, and heart and breathing rates increase, subconsciously obeying the mind's orders. About three hundred metres from the hole, they stopped, and listened, just as they had earlier, thirteen years ago.

"Sounds good from here," Herman smiled. "I can't hear a thing."

"Neither can I," agreed Kurt.

Herman quickened his pace, feeling in his gut that this time they would be more successful, and mentally imagined that the hole would be abandoned. It would be the simple secluded spot far from humanity, the place he remembered, and had dreamed about, a place where he and his brother could entertain themselves once more, in the splendour of the occasion.

NOPE!

As they crossed the plain, a disturbing sight came into view in the bushes above the river. "Look at that, Kurt." Herman pointed to the brown buildings, half-hidden in the bushes.

"Jeez, it looks like somebody's moved right in. I didn't know there was a road that even came close to this place." Kurt stared at the buildings, as they approached.

"Look up in the hills there." Herman pointed. "Bad enough last time that there were two guys who had fished the place dry. This time we hit civilisation."

Kurt looked to where his brother gestured. "It's a darn ski lift," he exclaimed. He paused, mentally trying to slap his memory into wakening. "I read that some people were going to build a ski development out here, but I didn't realise that this was the exact spot. Now I feel kind of stupid."

"Oh yeah." Herman gave his brother the 'I knew you were stupid,' look that can only follow such an admission. "Don't worry, we can still go fishing. It's just that we could have driven here. Didn't need that long walk."

"Fair enough. I guess next time when we come, it won't take quite as long."

(Fate, that sometime cruel ogre, (or ogress) had dealt poor Herman another low blow. This time it was not an enemy fisherman that became the foe. This time it was the encroachment of humanity itself. Thirteen years is a long time, and things do happen. The spot was such a superior one, that indeed, without the very-locals recognising it, the hills here were longer than anywhere else along the Battle's whole course, having seduced a developer type to build a ski hill. The 400-foot vertical drop and the nature of the surrounding hills provided a most suitable spot. The development had happened over 4 or 5 years, unbeknownst to Herman, or his brother.

What it did mean is that they had done a whole lot of hiking for nothing. The road into the ski hill development came within about 30 yards of Herman's 'secret' hole, transforming it into much less of a secret. Perhaps it was still a secret to those who did not know there were fish lurking in those shallow waters. Of course the real 'secret' lay somewhere in the brotherly camaraderie, and had naught to do with fish)

Kurt took a look around, and did the proper Canuck thing, to have a deserving laugh at his own folly. "Shoot," he uttered to his brother, "I guess we could have saved a little time."

"Like only about an hour," replied Herman, sarcastically, "and we get to walk back up that hill, too. You always bring me bad luck."

"You're making me feel guilty now," suggested Kurt. "You want me to go get the truck, and drive around? It's probably about twenty miles. You can stay here and fish."

"No. That's okay," smiled Herman. "We might as well be skunked already, though. But jeez, I need more exercise."

Together they walked down to the edge of the river and set about casting out in search of the great great grandchild fish of the walleye that had gotten away on them in childhood. A few casts later, and Herman had one on. He reeled it in, and lifted the poor thing out of the water, in the same manner that small children lift yellow perch up. It was a walleye all right, at least five inches long.

"Hey Brother, you caught one!" Kurt choked it out with false enthusiasm, restraining himself from making the obvious shots about the fish's size.

Herman flipped his rig, and the tiny walleye came off, and flopped back in. "I think we should come back again in thirteen years. This guy might just be a little bigger then, eh?" he smiled.

"I'm up for it," said Kurt. "At least we can drive here then. You won't be able to walk down that hill anyway. You'll be like 97 then."

"It's a deal, Brother. Maybe you'll bring me some better luck."

How to Lose a Canada Day Canoe Race

Someone had the insightful brainstorm in early 1967 to celebrate 100 years of Confederation by having a canoe race between Hardisty and Fabyan, along the Battle, through Camp Wainwright. These gifted idea makers created a poster announcing the wonderful event, met to compile and sort out the rules, found sponsors who would offer up a colossal cash prize, and solicited judges and officials to volunteer. Lo, it would be a joyous and majestic affair, celebrating local ingenuity, fur trade, and competition, all in one mighty illustrious ordeal. Of course there was no other choice. To not celebrate would only show disdain for the country. Canuck pride had towns competing against one another to see who could celebrate the centennial most grandly. Other creative outcomes included giant tin Easter eggs, UFO landing-pads, and sordid other projects to 'put this town on the map'. The end results became reasons of pride or ridicule or both. All the glorious schemes at least aided in establishing local identities, and provided topics for coffee-shop discussion.

These bright propositions always end up, somehow, in labour for a lot, and attention for a few. Such division of labour analysis of the concept was not in the minds of the entrants. Would-be-canoeists that noticed the poster, although they glanced at all the words, only cognised one sentence: "Winning Team - $500."

Organisers, being organisers, were sure to encounter some adversity. Foresight is never the forte of some. (In fact, it is a forte of few, and the demise of many.) Yet ideas become reality, and this one did. Lack of organisation is especially true whenever the scheme is a 'first', for there is no way to learn from previous mistakes. The Battle itself was one example of the adversity silently beckoning, because its geography is quite deceptive.

Well, the lure of easy gold is a wondrous thing. Five hundred bucks is five hundred bucks. Five hundred 1967 dollars would compare to 2000 of today's. No wonder more than one pair of eager-for-the-easy-buck men (and women, too) entered the affair, their hearts set on the cash. One such pair, high school students, was Benny and Doug.

Benny lived by the river so figured that, by itself, gave him a distinct advantage, much akin to home court advantage. Now, Benny wasn't the brightest fellow, so he needed all the advantages he could get. He was just one of those schemer/dreamer types that invent, or write, or otherwise kill their time with useless daydreams of no benefit to society, other than to entertain their compatriots in schemehood. Not that that does not serve a purpose. Where would this world be without its bullshitters, connivers, and inventors? Besides, occasionally one of them does luck on to brilliance. Then the rest have something to look up to, or envy.

Of course, Benny had a plan for procuring the five hundred bucks. What self-proclaimed entrepreneur wouldn't? Benny's initial concept involved venturing out into the valley the day before the race, to hide a small outboard about five miles downstream from the start line, just around some bend in the river. Then, when racing dreams became reality, he, and partner Doug (not McKenzie) would work their shoulders off in the milieu of the start, and gain a lead. Once the outboard's hiding spot was reached, they would scramble to the shore, and retrieve it. After firing it up, they could then be gas-powered to within a few miles of the finish line. At another pre-selected hiding spot, they would ditch the cheater's tool, and coast to victory, looking as though they had been in training for several years for the event, in true voyageur style.

"How do you know where to place the motor?" Doug wasn't about to participate in this, unless he had some assurances that the plan was somehow nearly sure to succeed. This was heady stuff for him. He wondered why Benny had 'selected' himself, for a canoe race. A three-hundred-pound out of shape laze somehow didn't seem fitting of voyageurism, even temporarily.

"I know the country down there by Hardisty well. We've skidooed it in winter, and we've trapped beaver along there. Besides, you could hide a motor anywhere, basically. Just as long as you and I are far enough ahead of everyone else." Benny could always make his knowledge sound better than the facts. (But is that not one of the wondrous delights of youth?)

"And how do you propose that we ensure that?" Doug was less confident, for he had seen other Benny-dreams backfire. For now, as this was all talk, there was no point in questioning Benny's selection of mates. Most likely, it was because he was Benny's only friend, for previous schemes had backfired, and Benny's continual yapping had turned others off.

"We practice, Stupid. We practice. Canoeing is really easy. You have canoed before, haven't you?"

"No, not actually," Doug confided, "but I've watched it."

Benny explained. "Well, it's really easy. All you need is strong arms. If you come out to my place once or twice, we'll practice a bit, and then I'll do the rest. Just getting the motor out there, and then picking it up. This will be real easy, I tell you. I'll even split the five hundred bucks with you."

"You mean you weren't going to before?" Doug sounded surprised. It seemed to him that if he did half the work, he should receive half the benefit.

"You have to admit that it is *my* idea." Entrepreneurs are entrepreneurs. Fair play may not always be at the forefront of the profit-making scheme. That means sometimes profits can come ahead of friendships.

"Sure, but without a partner, you wouldn't be able to do it at all. And from some of the other weird ideas you've had, I'm not so sure that you'd be able to find anyone else to enter with you. I still am not sure that you and I can get such a head start to be out of sight of all those other guys." Doug doubted that the canoe could be very streamlined with him sitting in the front of it. It seemed pretty dozy, the whole plan, but on second thought, most anything is better than thinking about school.

Benny smiled. "So you're in, eh? None of the other teams will be so stupid as to work really hard at the beginning. They will all be saving their energy for the long haul, and it will be a long haul, I can assure you. That river winds back and forth forever. In our case, because we are just kids, others will think we're stupid, no one will be surprised to see us take off fast. There are some very sharp bends in the river. It's easy to get out of sight."

"Yeah, I guess so. I guess the worst case is I can be out the ten buck entry fee, but I'll still get to see some river." Doug remained sceptical, but what the heck, the world needs its follow-along suckers, just as it needs its dreamer-schemers. There is a place for one and all.

"Right on. I'll go down today after school and sign us up. Gimme your ten for the entry." Benny reached out his arm, with his hand turned up. There was only slight hesitation as Doug retrieved his wallet from his back pocket, and pulled a crisp ten from it.

"Ask them how many other people have entered, out of curiousity, okay? Since tomorrow is the deadline, we'll know how many other people we have to beat. Hopefully there won't be very many." Doug secretly hoped he and Benny would be the only ones.

Alas, such was not the case when the next day at noon hour, the entrepreneur mates drove down to the town office to peruse the posted entry list.

Doug read the list of names, then turned to Benny. "Shoot, there's about fifteen entries. Most of these guys I haven't even heard about. Some of them I know are hockey players. Some are probably soldiers from Camp. Some sound like Indian or Metis names. Probably guys that canoe all the time. There might even be one or two teams from somewhere like Edmonton who have practised. They're probably in shape, not like you and me."

"Stop worrying, will you," Benny commanded. "Fifteen is small. There could have been fifty. There's no such thing as natives who canoe all the time. That was in the old days, you idiot! We have my secret plan, remember? There's no way those guys can out-paddle my little outboard. If they can, they are true voyageurs."

"You mean if we get to the motor spot before they do, and they don't notice?"

"Stop worrying. Do you want to drop out?" Benny gazed at his buddy. Whenever he sensed doubt, he always gave these ultimatums. It was a psychological strategy becoming of would-be leaders and politicians.

"No. That's not what I meant. I just don't want to look like an idiot." Doug was not as used to looking like an idiot as was his friend, and the prospect of joining idiothood was not one which he inwardly approved of. His stature because of the obesity was already in jeopardy. Still, he had more friends than Benny. Certainly within the peer-pressured confines of high school, he didn't want to lower his social status. A failure at an event like this could be downright disastrous. In fact, he was already at risk for mere association with this fellow. He'd noticed how some of the others walked right by, not even bothering to say, "Good morning."

Benny was not one to be discouraged, though. He held the distorted 'I cannot fail' attitude that is so commonplace amongst youth. Fortunately, Doug's comments were having some affect, which got him to thinking, "If Doug is right, and he can't canoe very well, then we just may be out the twenty bucks. That would be unfortunate, a disappointing scar on my credibility, not to mention my ego." (As if the fellow had *any*. Credibility, that is.)

On the way home from high school that day, he contemplated ways that he and Doug might further their advantage. Purchasing a better canoe was out of the question. So was going into hard training. They were both far too lazy for that. Three weeks was not a long time to get into shape, especially for his out of shape friend. No doubt it would help to do some canoeing practice with the fellow, especially entering the water. The rules had said that the start would be from land. If they could enter quickly, that would help. Friend Doug was not quick, but not as slow as his appearance suggested either. His lumbering was deceptive, like a football lineman's.

As Benny crossed the bridge, he decided to stop for a moment and contemplate this river. Perhaps the river itself would provide him with some additional clues as to how he could outsmart the others. That five hundred dollars could buy a lot of beer, or maybe even impress some chicks, and his dad had always taught, "Where there is a will, there is a way." (He had distorted the saying to, "When there is a bill (cash) there is a way.") Therefore he remained optimistic, even though it seemed that he and buddy Doug perhaps had bitten off more than together they could chew, now that they had seen the entry list.

As he stood on the bridge watching the springtime high water flow gush beneath him, it occurred to him just how curvy this river was. He recalled that just north of Hardisty, it was even more filled with switchbacks, than here. What he needed was an aerial photograph, or a detailed map of the river. "Surely," he surmised, "there is a place where a short portage will increase our time dramatically. It's enough probably that we have a motor, but if it breaks down, a short-cut will absolutely ensure our prosperity."

He woke occasionally throughout the night, seeing himself and his friend being presented the cheque at an awards ceremony. Often the musing was of dragging the canoe up a bank, hustling across a short grassy flat, canoe in tow, and then crashing back down the bank to the water. His sleep was restless, and he hoped that sufficient planning would increase his confidence over the next few days. Waking up each night, planning the methods for obtaining this free cash was not something he looked forward to. His days would be days of yawning if that were the case, and when the race day arrived, he would be plain exhausted, unable to paddle at all.

Before school the next day, he met Doug. "Hey, Man, I have even a better plan yet."

"I am not surprised," answered Doug, who wasn't surprised. He wished now that he hadn't volunteered himself so readily, and had spent *his* night thinking of ways he could get out of this. In the end, if things didn't start looking up, he could always feign injury. Either that, or find someone dumber than himself, to take his place. That might be difficult. Feigning injury seemed the more likely scenario. It would be his last resort to save grace. A sore back might be just the thing to get him out of the mess. Unless of course, the plan actually succeeded.

"We need to go downtown to the county office to get a map," Benny continued.

"Okay, Man, whatever you say. But what good is that going to do us?"

"Well, what we'll do is, instead of practising canoeing so much, is, we are going to skip school one afternoon, and go down by Hardisty, and find a spot on the river where there is a good shortcut, across land. You know that that river has a lot of switchbacks, don't you?"

"Yeah, you can see that from the top of the valley in a lot of places. Does this mean that you've given up on the idea that we're going to use a motor?" Doug could not believe how serious this guy was about taking the cheating way to five hundred dollars.

"Oh, no. Not at all. I still want to use the motor. You don't really want to paddle all the way, do you?"

"No, of course not. I didn't volunteer so that I could get all tired."

"This way it's absolute that we will win. Either thing on it's own would be enough. This way we will have two advantages, the portaging shortcut, or shortcuts, and the motor."

"And just how do you intend to get a map that will show us all the switchbacks?" asked Doug.

"Don't worry. You worry way too much. Today at noon, you and I will go downtown to the MD office. They have maps like that there, because they want to know who owns all the land around. Dad has one at home, but I didn't want to steal it, and it didn't show all the way down to Hardisty. That's a different MD. But they'll probably have one here in town."

"Well, it does sound like a plan. I'm not so sure about skipping school, though."

"Jeez, the more we talk, the more I think that you don't want that five hundred bucks."

"Okay. Okay. I'll come." Doug could just not bring himself to share in his friend's expectancy of the cash. He thought it was somewhat distorted from the reality of the situation. He figured their chances were realistically about one in a hundred. It seemed to him that Benny fully expected to win. However, he had nothing much else to do.

When the bell rang, they headed outside. As they passed a couple of sexy young females, they overheard condescending voices, saying, "Did you hear those two are in that canoe race?" Benny and Doug ignored the giggles that followed.

The duo drove down to the MD office, and purchased a map that showed the detailed path of the Battle. It was even more twisted than they expected. Near Hardisty, there seemed to be endless switchbacks. Selecting the right ones would take time, and they had also to consider the view from roads. What if a spectator should view the pair running across some field, canoe in tow? Wouldn't that person be obliged to report the skulduggery to the judges? To lose fair and square held some honour, but to lose from disqualification would possibly mean even greater embarrassment.

It bothered Doug more than Benny. "You know, I don't want to get caught cheating."

"Don't worry. Look at this map. There are hundreds of places to portage. Besides, you don't even know if it's illegal." Benny was tiring of his friend's constant doubting. Perhaps he should have found a different partner. It seemed to him now that Doug almost wanted to lose.

Doug, hoping that some good would come of this, suggested, "Well, then, let's go look at the rule posting again. I didn't read it real carefully. Did you? Maybe it's legal to portage. Maybe those contest inventors didn't think of all that. They didn't seem too bright to me."

A careful reading of the posted rules answered their questions:

Rule 6: Once a canoe is in the water, it can not be removed until it crosses the finish line. Rest breaks on shore will be allowed, but there will be absolutely no portaging, or shortcutting across land.

Rule 8: No mechanical devices such as small outboard motors will be allowed.

"Well, there goes that plan." Doug looked at his friend.

"Not at all. How are the judges going to know? There is no way that they will be able to put judges all the way along. That would take about 500 people. And there's no way they can put in a motorboat. The river will be far too shallow for that. All we have to do is make sure no one sees us portage, and no one sees us with the motor. Then it's a sure deal."

"Well, not quite," added Doug. "We also have to make sure we get a quick lead."

"Oh, you're right, but you can come out on Saturday, and we'll practice entering the river a lot. Some stroking, too, so you'll at least know some of the basics."

41

"What do you mean, basics? I thought canoeing was just paddling a dumb boat. You mean there are better ways? I don't believe it."

Benny explained, "Sure. You can actually take courses on canoeing. Mostly it's just experience though."

The next day over lunch, the brainy guy and his brawny partner took the map to a park, and considered it carefully.

"So are we still going to try to get ahead of everyone first, or do you think that's possible?" asked Doug.

"When I really think about it, I think it's possible. I mean, some of those guys are experienced canoeists, and others are hockey players in shape. You and I are just two ordinary guys. But they will all be saving energy. You and I will just go all out, right from the start. I was looking at the map last night, and it looks like there's a spot to portage, too. The river really winds back and forth a lot. It looks like you can save at least five miles right here." Benny pointed to the spot on the map that he had picked. "What we can do is hide the motor there, too. Then we can kill two birds with one stone."

Doug considered the map. His face evolved into a confident one the more he studied it. "I think you're right. This is a long way from any roads, too. The only problem I can see is that the portage might be totally bush. Then it'll be tricky. Hopefully it'll be a plain, and the banks are not too steep right there. That will be the tough part to figure out. I guess you're right. We are going to have to skip school one afternoon, and drive down there. That's the only way we'll know. Then if it's a good spot, you can get the motor there the day before the race. It looks like it's only about a mile walk from the nearest road. There's probably some guy's pasture we can drive into, anyway, to get closer."

Benny looked at his friend admiringly, "Wow, I'm surprised. You're finally changing your tune. I told you it was a remarkable plan. You're making me feel better now. For awhile there, I thought you were going to quit on me, and we wouldn't even be in the race."

"So when should we skip school?" Doug continued to demonstrate his newly found confident eagerness.

"Let's go when we don't have a teacher that will check attendance really close. That way our parents will never know we skipped. I hate having to explain stuff like that to them."

Doug reflected for a moment on their schedule, "This Thursday, then. We have Mr. Thomas. And on Saturday you can come over, and we'll go down to practice entering the water."

"Fine by me. We can talk about how we're going to spend that prize money, all the way to Hardisty, and back." Benny enjoyed postulating the sure-fire win.

Thursday arrived. When the bell rang at 11:50, the duo hustled out to Benny's truck, knowing that they would only have about three hours to check it out, if they were to be able to not arouse suspicion from parents.

The road to Hardisty seemed short, as Benny drove faster than he should have, but rural youth have heavy feet, and speed in half-tons was the custom of the day. Doug studied the map for the correct turnoff road that would lead them to the intended site, now labelled, in their minds, and on the map 'the cheater's paradise' by the unscrupulous pair. On the map was a crudely drawn circle. If someone should see the map, it might tip off the plan.

Benny turned left off the main road, following his navigator's instructions, and travelled along a less travelled dirt road for another mile or so, watching for a gate into a pasture, all the while. There appeared to be no entry, so they stopped, got out, and headed off on foot in the direction of the river, map in hand.

"You know, what we really needed was our own small airplane. That would have been a lot less complicated. We could have scouted this out in a few minutes," Benny observed.

"Jeez, you dream big. I never think of that kind of stuff," admired Doug.

Soon they arrived in sight of the river, at an abrupt bank that they had to scramble down. Doug did more roll-and-crash than scramble, certainly scaring off any birds, beavers, or deer in the area. The selected portage shortcut was on the opposite side of the river. They sauntered along until they found a spot where crossing was an effortless matter, by the simple pulling off of shoes and socks, and rolling up of pant-legs. "Just don't get the map drenched," Benny reminded his crony.

They didn't have to scramble up the other side, as it was more beach-like, gently rising to a plain, and some thicket above. They found a well-traversed cow-path through the bushes. After about fifty yards, the trail returned close to the river, where the Battle flowed westward, and curved southward, indicating that its path around this switchback must indeed be long, as the map indicated. "Boy, this is good. Real good," remarked Benny. "We can increase our lead easily right here. No one will be able to spot us. The river will be down more by then, too, so the other racers will all be going slow. All we have to do is make sure they are all out of sight, and we can just scurry up across here, along the cow-path, and 'Voila!' That five hundred is ours for sure."

The cheater-duo headed back to the truck, having convinced themselves wholeheartedly of the validity of their scheme. Benny beamed as they drove off. "Only eighteen more days to go. Let's go and check out the start line place, so we can practice on a place that is a lot like it is. For this plan to work, it's essential that we get off to a remarkable start, ahead of all of the others. We can take a gander at the current, too. This river is so small that the current varies a lot from one side to the other. I think you're always better on the outside edge of a curve. Not everyone will know that. Some guys will take the shorter but slower way."

The young men drove on to check out the starting area, and then spent two full Saturdays practising. By the time race day arrived, they were beyond ready, fully prepared to earn, if somewhat dubiously, the reward. Doug spent his school days dreaming of huge mounds of chips and gravy he would be able to purchase with his $250 share. Benny thought of asking Amy out to a movie. Both of them only daydreamed, and neither *really* planned anything. Surely, something had to go wrong. Mostly the fun was in the effort.

The amazing day of the canoe battle arrived. Doug got a timely morning lift from his father to Benny's place, and together they loaded the canoe into the truck, for the haul to Hardisty. Race organisers were to provide a bus for the participants to return to the start point to retrieve vehicles. The organiser's had become more orderly, as they responded to participant's questions in the days leading up to the affair. It seemed that the number of organisers now far outnumbered the number of participants. A crowd of some hundred friends and relatives of racers had gathered to give the competitors a royal send-off. It was 100 years of Confederation, after all. Start time was 7 AM, and no one had any idea what the finish time would be. The officials would work both ends of the race, knowing full well that they would get to the Fabyan campsite far ahead of any racers. Many a person supposed how long it would take. Estimates varied anywhere from three or four hours, to some as high as twelve.

Benny and Doug only saw one outcome: they were certain to be first.

As planned, Benny had come out the night before, and carried the motor to its hiding spot, making sure it was loaded with gas. He had also gone on down to where he and Doug would begin the shortcut, and taken another look, just to be sure. In these endless switchbacks, a lot of the river looks the same, and he wanted to make double sure that he had the right spot. He had broken off a tree branch to mark the site, just for good measure.

By 6:30, the fifteen teams of competitors had lined up along the edge of the river, jostling about for the finest spot. The judges had decided to have the race start from land, so that it would be fair. Starting the race in the water would just be too difficult, mostly due to the current. Benny and Doug selected a spot in the middle of the pack, and nonchalantly prepared themselves. To onlookers with gambling eyes, it would appear that they would be the least likely to succeed. Particularly Doug was unimpressive, obviously so overweight, and out of shape. Neither young man looked like he cared much, dressed in jeans, and looking bedraggled, as if they had just awaken from slumber. Appearances were deceiving, and this was just more of the duo's plan.

"It's better to appear that we don't know what we're doing," Benny had planned, aloud.

They had discussed strategy on the way down. "We need to be unnoticed," Benny reiterated, "yet we need to make it look at least like we are trying some."

Doug reassured his pal. "Don't worry. With all of our practice, even if we don't get right out there first, we'll surely overtake the leaders. I feel confident. Don't you?"

"Sure, Doug. I'm always confident," Benny lied. In truth, the degree of confidence in each member of the pair had reversed. Doug was now the confident one, with all the planning, and Benny had come back to earth, as was his pattern. The closer he got to reality, on these things, the more accurat his perception became. Turning optimism into pessimism was his speciality.

At exactly seven, to a rousing cheer, with the apparent importance equivalent to the start of the Olympic 100 metres, an official, decked in a white suit and tie, fired the pistol into the morning air. They were off! In a hectic chaotic mess, the fifteen canoes were shifted, lugged, pushed, and dragged into the mighty Battle. Benny and Doug ran right out into the water, further than all of the others, and climbed aboard their vessel simultaneously, appearing to the spectators as if they had actually practised this part. The soon to be rich duo emerged from the scramble in second place, and by working hard, were soon ahead of the pack.

An old-timer who had come to watch them off, observed Doug and Benny working so hard, and whispered to the guy beside him. "Gee, those two sure are going to be tuckered. Something tells me they will probably be dead last. The big guy is sweating already."

Benny had Doug sitting at the front of the ship. He paddled from the back as an expert might, giving his lazy companion instructions on how to canoe all the while. From his seat in the rear, he could control at least the direction, and remain in the fastest current, compensating for Doug's dumbness, and the canoes forward slant. It didn't take long for them to be out of sight of the others. Within the first five twists of the river, they were nowhere to be seen.

"Come on, Doug! We gotta get further out." Benny spoke to his companion at the front of the canoe. "We have to get to the portage spot relatively quickly. We can't go slow at all. No one can see us when we jump out of the water."

Doug heeded the helmsman's advice and paddled harder. He lost more moisture from sweat than a back-catcher on a scorching hot day. At about 7:30 they arrived at the portage, and engine retrieval spot. There were no other canoes in sight to their rear. A quick scamper along the cow-path, and grabbing of the motor, had them back into the river in less than five minutes. Doug's strength was actually advantageous here, as the canoe was quite heavy. They were now at a spot in the competition that they felt for sure was in the lead, by a substantial distance, too. Doug mellowed, and stretched back. He reached over the canoe's side, and splashed handfuls of water on his face, and chest. His pal guided the canoe along with the aid of the side mounted gas engine. The five hundred bucks was only a few hours away!

This part was simple. Doug's task of navigator, besides gawking at the secret map they had, was to keep eyes and ears open for people. Likely spots for this inconvenience had already been agreed upon during the planning stages in the days prior to now. If Doug should see any onlookers upstream, he was to signal immediately, and Benny would shut off the engine, and hide it under his jacket in the bottom of the canoe. Then the pair would make like racers again until clear of the observers. The duo had considered the likelihood of this occurring to be slim. Perhaps somewhere near the start line where the Battle approached the road it would be likely. But that place was avoided altogether by their cheating portage. Certainly throughout Camp Wainwright, spectators were unlikely due to inaccessibility. Near the finish, there were a few roads, between the railway trestle, and the campsite finish area.

Doug was more relaxed than ever, and ecstatic about the money. "You know, Benny to tell you the truth, I'm surprised. It seems like this plan of yours is actually going to work."

Benny gleamed from the compliment, trying not to sound that he himself was surprised. "What did I tell you? If you can't trust Benny, who can you trust, eh?"

"So do you think there will be anyone near the railway bridge?" Doug was still refining the plans.

"Probably. I think that we are so far ahead by now that we could paddle the rest of the way anyway. I was going to ditch the motor about a mile past the trestle. I drove over there a couple of days ago and found a good spot."

"Didn't your Dad notice that the motor was gone?"

"No, it's stored out in a shack with all the other water stuff. He hasn't used it in a long time. I'm the only person who ever goes in there, so I know he doesn't know. Even if he did know, he'd probably just laugh."

"Well, that's good. My dad would be upset. He's so honest. I'll have to shut up about this for years. You too. You know, we can't brag about it to anyone." Doug knew that Benny was prone to boasting, and felt obliged to remind him whenever he could.

"Yes, Doug, I kinda had that figured out," Benny replied sarcastically.

They rounded a corner and the railway trestle came into view. "There's the railway," Doug informed Benny, the motor operator.

Benny reached over to shut the motor off, and put in into the canoe. "Well, get your oar going up there. We want to make ourselves look good." He reminded Doug.

Sure enough, there were a couple of people on the bridge. It was by far the best vantage point around.

The friendly people waved as the canoe passed underneath. "I hope they didn't see the motor," claimed Doug, in his paranoid way. "That would stink."

As soon as the twosome got around the next corner, Benny suggested, "We'd better pull to shore, and ditch this engine now. It's not a whole lot further to the campsite. Some other people may have wandered upstream."

"Okay," agreed the cheerful, but relieved buddy. They manoeuvred the canoe to shore, and Benny headed, motor in hand, for the bushes. He selected a secluded willow patch, and dropped it off, making sure it was well out of sight from anyone on the river. As long as some other competitor didn't stop here for a washroom break, the secret was totally safe.

Within about fifteen minutes, the pair could see the final destination ahead. They recognised some of the same people that had been at the start line. The official looking dude who had fired the gun was front and centre. "Well, we made it,

Brother," declared Benny. "Let's just try to pretend we're really tired."

The official stuck out his hand to congratulate Doug as he stepped from the front end of the canoe. "Congratulations, Son," said the suited man. "You and your friend here must be some kind of excellent canoers. Nice race."

After several more handshakes all around by spectators, and friends, they pulled the canoe up and over on to the grass, beside some trees, and out of hearing range of everyone. "I wonder how long we'll have to wait," pondered Doug.

"Well, I'm sure they probably want to give a speech or something. At least Suitman over there will. He looks the political type. My guess is we'll have to wait until everyone gets in. But we've waited three weeks already. Another three hours isn't going to kill us. So tell me, Man, are you surprised?"

Doug looked at his friend reflectively, "Well, to tell you the truth, yeah, I am surprised."

"Ha ha," Benny chuckled, "I figured you didn't trust me all along. And I kept telling you it was going to be like stealing candy from babies."

"So how do you plan to spend your dollars?" Doug had never really asked, and hadn't thought about it much. He hadn't actually figured on winning.

"I think I'll ask Amy out to a movie. The fact that we won this race is going to change a lot of things." Benny looked forward to any event from which he could boost his social status within the school. He usually acted like he didn't know, but he *knew*.

"Really? You don't actually think that she'll go out with you, do you?" Doug sounded surprised, both at his friend's new found confidence, and that he actually thought Amy, the one with those awesome legs, would indeed go out with him.

"Yeah. Really I will. The worst she can say is no. Maybe some day I will get her to come canoeing with me. Then I'll have a real canoeist partner." The gentle jibes continued.

"Okay, okay. Good luck. I'd like to bet that she won't go out with you, but hey, this plan worked, and I didn't think it would, so who am I to say?"

"So are you tired?" Benny was, and offered up the question as a hint that they lie in the grass for a doze. The fresh air had been tiring. So had the exercise. He couldn't imagine paddling the whole way.

"Yeah. I think I'll stretch out. If I fall asleep, wake me up when it's time to get the money." Doug leaned back on the grass, and eased his 300 pounds down, pulled his hat down over his eyes, and shut them. He breathed a heavy sigh, now that this ordeal was almost complete.

Outwardly, the unsteady sounds of haphazard snoring, coming from under the Edmonton Eskimo hat, indicated the big boy was getting some much needed rest.

Inside that lug of a head, it was an entirely different matter. Afternoon naps, especially ones after physical exertion, and excitement, can be rather interesting, even for apparent dullards. He began to dream, a daymare:

He was sitting at the breakfast table, staring at a huge mound of bacon and eggs. Other than the distorted quantity of food in front of him, the setting was realistic. The relationships too were normal, until Dad looked at him, with a look that wasn't Dad's customary look. It was the one that revealed, "I know you've been up to something, Doug."

He turned to look at his father. Father's ears, which were larger, and more mangled than normal, more like Prince Charles', perked up, like a dog's. "Do you hear *that,* Doug? I wonder what that could be?" His tone was clear. Father knew exactly what it was, and revenge was upon him.

'*That*' was the sound of sirens. The pair of them moved to the front door to see if it was just sirens on the highway, or if the sirens were headed for their place. Sweat started seeping out of Doug's armpits, and all along his back, both in the dream, and in real time. Four black and white police cars, lights flashing, sirens blaring, larger than normal police cars, magnified about double, to the size of gravel trucks, came roaring up. The tires slipped on the gravel as they halted. In unison, eight burly linebacker types, even larger, came marching forward. They were caricatures, not real, like the distorted ones you might see in a political cartoon.

The sweating increased, as the leader asked, "Where is he?" in the gruffest, roughest, toughest voice imaginable, more akin to a wolf's growl, than a man's questioning.

Dad did not speak at all. He stepped back, away from his son, and merely pointed, with his enlarged forefinger, which was now the size of a long English cucumber, directly at Doug's head. All parental loyalty had disappeared. There was no unconditional love here, only pure disdain, and a glare of total disappointment, which could only mean banishment from the nest for life.

The eight hideous black-uniformed beasts, faces now remade to wolves' heads, both fangs gleaming, each armed with those sharp pointed cave man clubs, approached, from eight directions, encircling the victim. He could not distinguish if they were headhunters, wolves, sharks, eagles, or cops. He recognised the vibration clearly enough. Something out of the ordinary whose sole purpose for existing was to evoke fear in cheaters.

"I'll go. I'll go!" He screamed.

He jolted backwards, as he felt the firm hand on his shoulder. His eyes sluggishly opened, and there were no police, thankfully. It was just Benny. "Hey Man, you were snoring, and talking in your sleep something awful. It's time to get up. They're gonna give us the money."

Doug shook his head, after standing, and smoothed his sweat-covered brow with his hand. He knew that he wasn't looking exactly charming. The sun, the nap, and the daymare, had the combined effect of turning him from a somewhat obese fellow, into one ugly soaking sot, positively. He wished he could go shower before the presentation, and hoped his smell wouldn't have everybody backing away. There was no turning back, as Benny beckoned him toward the judge's

48

table where Suitman awaited. A crowd had gathered to congratulate all the participants, and especially the canoe race champions.

Suitman did the usual political stuff, thanking all the judges, the participants, the parents of the participants, the volunteers, the drivers, the parents of the drivers, and God for creating the river and birch trees. Doug just wished he'd hurry up, for he understood that really the guy was just boasting, as Suitman himself had organised the whole thing.

At the end of the speech, and after the presentation, Suitman suggested, "Perhaps the winners would like to say a few words."

Doug's gut suddenly reeled. It overwhelmed him. It was a sudden realisation, and so spiritual like, that he was compelled to act on it. To heck with his buddy. To heck with his pride. All *that* was tossed out the window, as he stepped to the podium, still in mental disarray from the dream, and from the insecurity about sweating. He had had a long day, and it was time to put things square.

"We cheated. We don't deserve the cheque." The words tumbled out. He thought he felt Benny's glare peripherally. In reality, Benny's face showed shock, then relief.

Suitman had a far heavier reaction. All was suddenly not perfect in the Kingdom of Battle Canoe.

Doug didn't say any more. He reached for the cheque from his pal, and gave it back to Suitman, leaving the poor organiser in a lurch, and with the unenviable task of redoing his speech.

But with time, and assistance from his assistant, he endured, and the team that had finished second accepted their rightful prize.

Benny and Doug trudged slowly off towards their canoe, looking like a cross between defeated soldiers, and forlorn puppies. The fifty yards was a long and lonely walk. At least the crowd hadn't started chanting, "Shame! Shame! Shame!"

Benny put his arm on Doug's shoulder, and without speaking, said, "It's okay. You did the right thing."

They heard someone approaching from behind. Together they turned, to greet the lovely female face of Amy, and her likewise gorgeous friend, Liz. "Hey, Guys, we just wanted to say that what you did back there was really impressive. Maybe we could buy you a pop or something when we get back to town."

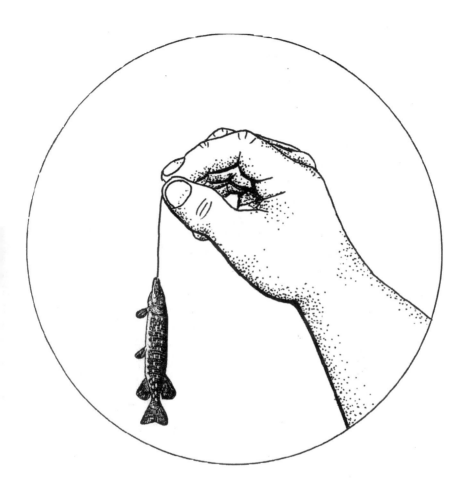

<u>Marvin's First Fish</u>

    The youthful questioning face below the locks of red hair stared up into its mother's. He moved his mouth adjacent to her ear, and whispered politely, but curiously, "Mom, what's wrong with that guy?" He was referring to the gigantic (to him), but proud and loud older fellow standing there on the other side of the campfire. He'd been closely keeping an eye on the scene for the last ten minutes.

    "Nothing, Dear. That's perfectly normal. You did that, too, probably."

    "Well, I sure can't remember being *that* excited." Jimmy looked at her again.

    "Oh, you probably were," she reassured him, "but now you're an experienced fisherman. Now it's different, eh?"

    "Yeah, I guess so. But jeepers, it's just such a little baby fish, too. My first fish was a lot bigger than that. His fish is nothing. Dad would've thrown it back."

"But it's his *first* fish, Dear."

"But, Mom, I've caught at least twenty fish, and none of them were that small, and I can't ever remember making such a fuss, even the first time. What's wrong with that guy?"

Jimmy's mom put her forefinger on her lips and gave him the 'shhh' look he'd seen before when he started asking questions about adults. He didn't really understand why Mom would only answer these questions the next day, or some time later. It bugged him if he couldn't remember to ask her about these troubling life-situation things.

He ventured forth questioning once more, this time whining at Mom's seeming lack of acceptance of his own wonderment at the bizarre sight across the flame, "But Mom, I've never seen a bigger uglier man, or a smaller fish."

Mom's look turned to a cold glare, and Jimmy realised that indeed, he'd better shut up, for good. He'd have to wait until tomorrow. Even then, she may not be able to answer or want to answer, for sometimes she simply didn't answer the questions. He had yet to figure out why, but trusted that she must have a worthwhile reason when she responded, "I don't know." The answer he really hated was, "I'll tell you when you're older." He remembered most of these, and made sure he asked them when he was older.

Then, sometimes he'd get the same response again: "When you're older." He wondered just how old he'd have to be some times. He figured maybe if she was on her deathbed. She at 90 years, and he at 60, he could sit there, and ask away. Just maybe then she'd answer. Then again maybe she wouldn't.

Marvin, the fellow still holding up the six-inch pike, looked around to find someone he hadn't shown yet. He noticed Jimmy standing beside his mother. "Hey, Son, did you see the fish I caught?"

Jimmy snuggled in closer to his mom's legs, afraid the weirdo was going to come around closer, and put the gored, partly dried fish closer, too. Jimmy's worst fears manifested. Weirdo came around. "I caught him right over there." Marvin said it for what seemed the dozenth time.

"I know." Jimmy looked up, still grasping his mom's leg for protection. "And it's your first fish, too, ain't it?"

"Yep. It sure is."

Mom didn't help him out much. "Well, Marvin, bring it over here. Jimmy wants to have a closer look." She enjoyed making her boy squirm a little, or sometimes a lot.

Jimmy gave her a quick glare, but knew that he'd better follow along on Mom's polite routine, or he'd be in for a scolding on the way home. Kids had to be polite, even if they were forced or coerced.

A week earlier, Marvin had been watching his own youngsters play ball and had struck up a conversation with Shorty, regarding fishing, and going down to the Battle. Marvin lived about twenty miles up and beyond the river, and hadn't even known, up til then, that fish existed in the thing. But Shorty had convinced him.

Farmers, being the friendly folk that they are, do not hesitate to make sure others have such experiences. Shorty extended the invitation, "Usually we go down to the mouth of the creek every Sunday afternoon. Why don't you come down with us? Bring along some grub. The kids can go swimming, and we can all try our luck at fishing. There are a couple of good spots along there. You'll see."

Marvin smiled. This wasn't something he nor the rest of his family had ever done, and it was cheap, so he accepted the invitation, not letting on to Shorty that he was excited. Fifty-year-old men are not supposed to get excited. His situation, of some tough luck on the farm, had brought some poverty with it, and such experiences were welcomed. Other folk went on longer holidays, and had a lot more stuff.

Marvin, and family, spent a few days looking forward to the experience, dumb as that sounds. But out here, even in the 60s there still existed a more pio-neerish folk or two. Hillbilly (although not quite appropriate, because these folk were no Jed Clampetts to the extreme) is still an apt way of describing such types.

To an outsider, all farmer folk may seem the same, but locals know that that's a myth. A half mile down the road can be as different as half way around the planet.

On Sunday, Marvin and household had driven to the mouth. Shorty right away volunteered his fishing outfit, and took an eager Marvin off to the water for a couple of casting lessons. As soon as Marvin had it figured out, Shorty returned to the campfire for the easy relaxed talk and bull with the others who had gath-ered.

In about fifteen minutes, heads were twisted all about in the direction of the huge burly fellow, as he whooped and hollered and yahooed his way back, with the stupid, but obviously too hungry, six-inch pike still dangling on the two-inch hook. Most of the adults and older folk in the crowd understood the fellow, sim-ple but good guy that he *was*. It was his first fish, and perhaps his only fish ever. At 50 years old, if a guy were to get married, and have a 'first' in that realm, it would be more exciting than if he's only twenty. Only little kids, and mostly only Jimmy, were bewildered by the fellow's reactions.

Marvin stuck out the fish closer so Jimmy could see. "It's a beautiful fish, isn't it, Son?"

Jimmy had seen a few fish. He'd seen walleye, yellow perch, and trout. This bleeding-from-the-gills six-inch scaly speckled wide-mouthed piece of muscle didn't qualify for beautyhood, in any way. Neither did the guy holding it. Jimmy's mother squeezed him a little, giving him the "Be polite!" message.

"Yes, Sir, that sure is a pretty fish you caught there." His tone was far from convincing, but Marvin didn't pick up on that.

"What are you gonna do with it, Mister?" Jimmy ventured.

"Well, I guess now that everyone has seen it, Shorty is going to show me how to filet it, and I'm going to eat it."

"Oh, that's good." Jimmy really meant this comment, as that might mean he wouldn't have to put up with watching this guy go on and on any more. At least he hoped.

"Do you want to come and watch us filet it, Son? Maybe you can learn something, too." Marvin held the assumption that others thought similarly, or were at least as inexperienced as he was. In short, he hadn't gotten around much. Little did he know that Jimmy had seen Mom or Dad filet all kinds of fish, and that this whole fish thing wasn't new to the boy.

Jimmy stared up. "No, I don't think so. I think I'll go swimming again." This satisfied Marvin, and he moseyed off to find his mentor, Shorty, so he could go acquire some more angler skill.

Jimmy looked up at his mom, and shook his head back and forth questioningly, indicating he still required some answers to this.

"Do you want to come with me for a walk along the river?" she asked.

He nodded appreciatively, as he knew that Mom was going to explain something to him, and he definitely wanted an explanation. This guy was almost inhuman.

Once they had gotten out of hearing range, Mom began, "You see, Son, the world is a big place. There are lots and lots of different people out there. Marvin hasn't ever had the chance to catch fish, like you have. So it was very special to him. Just wait. As you get older, you will surely meet people even stranger than Marvin. Actually he's nothing compared to some of the people I met during the war. The important thing is to see them all as people, and to always be polite."

"You mean Marvin's *never* been fishing before. I thought everyone went fishing." Jimmy couldn't believe it.

Jimmy's mother chuckled. "No, Son. Not everyone has been fishing."

"Really?" He looked at her, disbelieving.

She laughed at the whimsy in his innocence. "*I've* never caught a fish, Jimmy."

"But you're a girl, Mom. Girls don't fish."

She laughed. "This girl doesn't. That doesn't mean I couldn't. And lots of women do fish, although it seems to be more of a man thing."

"You've never caught a fish?" Still it hadn't sunk in.

"Some people just don't do things. I've never travelled outside Canada. I've never driven the grain truck, or the combine. Not everyone does everything, you know. Your Dad's never baked cookies, or rode on a motorcycle, like I have."

Jimmy's face lit, as he interrupted her, "You rode a motorcycle?"

She smiled, at his enthusiasm. "Yes, Dear. During the war."

"Wow, Mom! I didn't know that."

"The world's a big place, Jimmy. Are you figuring that out?"

"Yeah, I guess so." He smiled up at her. "I think I understand. Let's go back. I want to watch that weird fat man skin his stupid fish."

Mom stared rather harshly again. "His name is Marvin, Jimmy."

"Okay, okay. Marvin's fish, then."

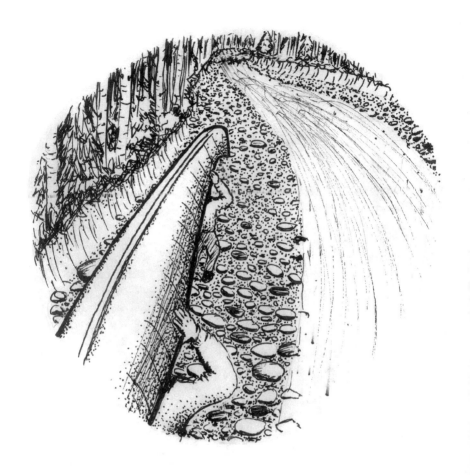

Mini-Deliverance

The humble creeks that flow into the Battle are even more insignificant than the Battle itself. They are basically glorified spring runoff streams at the bottom of scenic valleys. In rainy years, they flow all summer long. But even then, a leaper type kid can usually jump right across at the right spot. There is absolutely no danger, other than twisting your ankle, or inadvertently tripping and falling into the water, which is as much cattle manure as rainwater. In earlier times, beavers created dams here and there. In many years, these creeks dry up completely; a fact reinforced by the place names being 'Coulee' rather than creek.

One such typical creek is the Buffalo Creek, at the bottom of Buffalo Coulee. The steep coulee meanders back some thirty miles from the Battle River

Valley, and is home to several pastures, and meadows, and homes up on the adjacent hills. When the bottom of it is flat, the little creek wanders back and forth in even more twists than the Battle at its worst. Grattan Coulee, Meeting Creek, and Grizzly Bear Coulee are three other similar sites.

Lazyhead and Flipper had crossed the Buffalo on Highway 41 on numerous occasions. One of their witless childhood dreams was to hike it, or better yet, in springtime, canoe it. "You know, Brother," said Lazyhead, "some spring, when the water is up, we should canoe from here to its mouth." (A mile as the crow flies, 10 miles as the creek flows.) "We've been to the mouth, and you can see a lot of it from here, but there's a chunk in the middle, through those bushes, that I've never seen at all." (Most people cannot see through bush.)

"Yeah, that would be fun, if we *just* had a canoe," agreed Lazyhead. "Too bad we don't have one." The plugs for more toys got subtler with age. Father McAllister somehow ignored this one, too.

The canoe did happen along to the farm, circumstantially, as a gift from an old friend who had gotten tired of it, when the brothers were a bit more mature, about 13 or so. One day, on the way to town, about a week after a quick spring thaw, Flipper noticed the creek was substantially up. "So, Brother, you remember when we were kids (odd how 13-year-old kids remember themselves as kids) when we wanted to go canoeing down there. Looks like we could do it now."

"Yep, it sure does," agreed Lazyhead, as he looked at the flat valley to the east. The creek rambled back and forth, in the idyllic setting below the north side of the valley prairie hills, not quite yet in full crocus bloom.

Flipper turned to the driver of the truck, the wise one, and asked, "Do you think you can drop us off, Dad?"

In such cases it was 'do as requested', or put up with teenage whining for a while, so Father did as requested. It wasn't a big deal to throw the canoe on the pickup, then two hours later, go to the mouth of the creek, down another old road, and into a farmer's pasture, to retrieve the adventurous pair. "Sure. Not today, though. It'll have to be tomorrow."

This suited the boys just fine. "In fact, tomorrow's even better," agreed Lazyhead. "It'll give us some time to plan." Planning was one of Lazyhead's self-revealed strengths. This marvellous plan involved a whole lot. Put the canoe and the oars into the truck. The manifestation took five minutes, and the planning took two seconds. What he really meant was that it would give them time to daydream of the wondrous adventures they might come upon, in the mile long valley. Not much could happen. This would be no <u>Deliverance</u>, for there were no hillbilly types in these hills. Shucks, if they saw a cow, they'd be lucky. Not so in the case of dreamers. Dreamers see things others don't. Over time they become bullshitters. Often broke bullshitters, at that.

The night of dreams ended soon enough. The morning was a chilly one, with ice on the puddles. Over breakfast, the wise one advised, "If you two really still want to do that, you should at least go this afternoon in the middle of the day when it's warmer."

He was right, of course, in his common sense way. Although it was hard, dealing with their own impatience, they waited until after lunch, although some time was found in their busy Sunday morning schedule to load the canoe and oars onto the truck. The life jackets were left behind, out of common sense, as the creek was never more than twenty feet across. In fact they figured to be stuck on some of the sharper corners, with the canoe being too long to manoeuvre around the corner. Knowing this, gum rubber boots were the chosen footwear, as they calculated that they'd be in and out of the canoe a lot.

Father pulled off the road beside the short bridge at the bottom of the valley, and remained in the front as the two wrestled the canoe out the back. "I'll be there in about two hours to pick you up," he called, as he drove off home.

"This first part is going to take quite a while, eh?" pronounced Lazyhead.

"Yep, but I have a feeling that it'll get more interesting later on, once we get to the trees," replied the younger brother, Flipper, as they shoved off.

After half an hour of uneventful switchbacks, Flipper observed, "It's pretty boring, really. You can't even see anything down in here, in the channel. From the road, or anywhere up higher, you can at least see what's going on, or how far we've come."

"So why don't we stop, and climb up the bank? Then we'll be able to tell at least where we are, and how far it is until we get to bushes." Lazyhead's suggestion was the only way they could get an overall sense of where they were in the valley. The perception of things from the water, on a river, or this creek, is very limiting, especially so if the watercourse has immediate high banks. You get a fantastic specific view, but an unsatisfactory general view. They stopped the canoe, and clambered up the bank.

Flipper looked back some 300 yards to the bridge and highway where they had been dropped off. "Gee, we've hardly even come half way from the bridge to the trees. I'd have figured we'd have come a whole lot further than that by now."

"Yep, these switchbacks are really something. I think once we get to the trees, it'll straighten out a bit. Basically, it has to, because the valley itself gets a lot narrower. I've walked back up from the mouth a bit, and it's pretty straight there."

"Well, I hope so, because I think it's going to be longer than just two hours." Flipper never wanted to put his father out on these timing things. Unlike these two, Dad did have some important things to take care of. "So let's hurry up a bit," he suggested.

Soon the adventurers were amidst poplar bush. Flipper pulled his oar out of the water. "Listen. Can you hear that?" Together they heard the sound of gurgling water ahead. This could only mean that somehow the water was dropping over something. They rounded the next corner cautiously, to spot a foot high beaver dam blocking the creek. It was spring flow, and most of the creek splashed over in a yard wide tumble right in the middle of the dam.

"Pull in to shore," commanded Lazyhead.

Flipper did as he was told. "So what do you think? I sure don't want to dump it, but it wouldn't be that hard just to canoe over it."

"Let's get out and take a closer look, then." Flipper climbed ashore, and held the boat still for his brother. "I wonder how come we didn't see any beaver dams before."

"Brother, I think that just might have something to do with the surroundings. Beavers need trees. We were on open prairie before." Lazyhead was using his 'you're a stupid one' tone, and in this case, although often it wasn't appropriate, and led to battles, the tone today was somewhat justified.

Normally Flipper would have been upset, but when he looked around, he realised the older brother was correct. He moved close to the dam. He wisely changed the topic away from his stupidity. "I think if we just go over straight, nothing will happen. The front end would have to go under."

"Yeah, and it'll be fun, too," agreed Lazyhead, happy that his prediction of the trees being accompanied by more adventure had been accurate. They re-entered the canoe, and lined it up in the centre of the creek, and aimed for the midpoint of the main flow. The front end dipped some as they cruised over the foot-high precipice, and then swivelled end to end as it swished along the fast flowing water immediately below the dam.

"Yeah!" Flipper gave his victory shout at the completion of the remarkable rapid. Suddenly the pair had transformed into white-water canoeists racing in the Rockies. It wasn't Niagara, or Helmeken, but still it was a waterfall. A feat to be proud of.

The creek had turned into a new pattern, for them, in its narrowing. There were now far less switchbacks, and far more evidence of the work of beaver. The pattern was that every hundred yards or so, around only a corner or two, there would be another dam, and the water would widen into a pond, then accelerate as it approached the dam. It made for easy canoeing, as it was a simple matter to line the canoe straight in the centre of flow, and then just coast over.

The creek's bed narrowed, and the water's pace gradually increased overall. Portions of creek bed held gravel, and the canoe encountered a few rocks. At one spot the pair had to portage around an ice shelf that had yet to melt, as the water formed a tunnel under the ice. "If we go through there, we'll have to duck, and you can't see. We could get stuck." Flipper had convinced his brother of the necessary portage.

After running half a dozen or more beaver dams, the brothers became increasingly confident. This was turning into a fine afternoon, after all. It had been such a superb idea, this.

Then it happened! Overconfidence, the killer of Olympic or Stanley Cup hockey dreams, got them. A slightly higher than any before beaver dam, where water angled toward the bank as it went over, nailed them. The canoe floated over as it should, and caromed off the bank with the water flow, twisting sideways. Too far sideways, thus toppling the pair into the icy water. "Whoa!" screamed Flipper, as he hit, and scrambled up the far bank.

His older brother Lazyhead was right behind him in the scramble to safety and the Dryland, although he had suffered a worse fate, having gone right under.

"It's damn cold!" Flipper summarised the situation concisely. Decision time it was. And it needed to be quick. Either they head up the hill through the bushes to home, or they wander along the creek for about 500 yards to the mouth and wait for Father. "This was a dumb idea," he said, as he looked at Lazyhead. Flipper's wonderful afternoon had switched to a horrible one in two short seconds.

Lazyhead looked sympathetically back, "You're right about that. But it was your dumb idea, remember?" Lazyhead knew this 'blame the brother' routine too well. There were times when the pair got along, like so far today, and then there were times that they didn't, which usually ended in bruises and/or tears and/or parental intervention. Circumstances varied but each was adept at casting fault outward.

Instinctively, they kicked off the gumboots. Farm kids all develop this instinct. It comes from playing, "I dare you" with the water lever in puddles or sloughs. You wade cautiously in until the water seeps over the top. (This despite the fact the manufactures even place a red 'warning' line at the top of the boots.) Then you lose, and farm kids lose about 90% of the time. Having wet socks in springtime was old hat to the brothers.

"So which way should we go?" Flipper asked his brother, as he wrung out the socks, as best he could. He knew that with clothing, the dryer the better was the rule. He proceeded to take his jeans off to wring them out as well. Not fun in the +2 temperature, especially putting the frigid and clingy things back on.

"I think we have to head up the hill. It's probably going to be 45 minutes or so before Dad gets there. If we're lucky, we'll meet him on the road, on the way down."

"Well, I think we should go meet him by the creek, it'll be a much shorter walk." Flipper, soaked to the gills, had transformed from eager voyageur partner into unwilling argumentative shipmate, in one fine drenching.

Lazyhead already had his mind made up. "You go right ahead, Brother. Dad and I will pick up your frozen corpse, somewhere down there. Just stay in the open so we can see you. I tell you it's better to keep moving. Any idiot would know that."

"There you go, calling me an idiot again! It was your idea to go canoeing, and you should have had the common sense to portage around that last beaver dam."

Lazyhead wasn't about to lose this battle. "You moron! You were the one at the front of the canoe. Obviously the guy in the front of the canoe should be able to see what the water is like. He's the guy that's supposed to make those decisions."

"Well, I didn't know that. All along you had been bossing me around.

Flipper, do this. Flipper, do that. I'm sick of it! And now look what you got us into."

Lazyhead, by now had his wet pants back on, and was pulling his drenched sweater on as well. He had decided to leave the heavy jacket with the canoe. It would be a burden to the run, and he meant to run. "Well, Brother, I don't really care whose fault it is. I'm going. I don't care if you stay here and cry yourself to sleep, or if you go to the mouth, although you're so stupid you probably can't find it. I **am** going up that hill, and straight home as fast as possible. It's the only way. Only a total moron would go the other way." He started picking his way upwards through the bush, to the nearest patch of prairie.

Flipper's bottom lip came out. He was becoming more enraged by the second, and ready to lay another licking onto older brother Lazyhead. If he could catch him, that is. Being Irish twins, the physical spats were usually his to win, but the main problem was that generally Lazyhead could outrun him. In this case Lazyhead had a twenty-metre head start. "I'm gonna kill you!" Flipper muttered through the extended lip, as he pulled on the last boot, and started the hunt, up the hill.

The anger and the run from it only aided their joint survival. Lazyhead could not decide if he was running to save himself from the hypothermia or from the heat from Brother. Flipper didn't care. He just wanted to catch the bastard and show him with a fist that *he, Flipper*, was no moron. Once and for all!

So together they picked their way through the bushes, and patches of prairie to the top or the valley, to summerfallow fields and farmer trails along the fence-lines. Two locomotives heaving steam, and grunts. The body heat from the exercise did help, a lot. It was just a Godly benevolent thing it wasn't 40 below, or further than three miles.

Once up, out in the open, Flipper called ahead, "Wait up, Lazyhead! We can run together."

Lazyhead couldn't tell whether this was the ally in his brother or the foe, so he slowed his pace a little, waiting until the younger brother got really close, so he could read the eyes. Clearly, from the glare, it was still the foe, so he turned, and ran on, speeding up to regain the respectable safe lead, to the brother's revamped glare, from the getaway. Evidently, they had both been through this routine before.

After the third repeat of the 'almost-caught-me-but-not act', they came to the south road. The running was easier now, and there was less than a mile to the comfort of the kitchen. As the gruesome, wet, hopeless looking pair approached the gate, Dad's blue Ford pulled out, on his way to pick them up. This time he saved some gas.

It was a welcome sight for Lazyhead. It would have to be an extreme mad-on that Flipper had if it were to continue in the presence of the family referee. He opened the passenger door, and jumped in, sliding over to leave room for the angry one. When Flipper arrived, Father asked, "What happened?"

Flipper replied, "Stupid guy here dumped it on me. Then he ran away."

Father did not take long to have the situation assessed. Obviously they had gone under, and that had caused a fight. "Well, whatever happened, you both look a little tuckered." He gunned the truck, in reverse, back in the direction of the house.

Flipper reached over and pinched Lazyhead's right arm, tightly.

Lazyhead made sure that Dad really knew they were at it again. "Stop it, you idiot! We're home now. You should just be happy I saved your life."

"Look whose calling who an idiot! You're the one who thought of the stupid idea in the first place. Didn't he, Dad? You remember, don't you?" Now the competition was on to see who get the parent on his side.

Father proved to be smart, almost. "Well, I think you're probably right. I can't remember. You guys have both been talking about that trip for awhile. I suspected you wouldn't make it, though. I knew the creek got narrower and faster at the far end."

Lazyhead was not impressed. "Well, if you knew that, why in heck didn't you tell us?" Hey, perhaps, they could unite, and blame Father.

"You wouldn't have listened, anyway." Father Mac knew this to be true.

Flipper cut in. "Well, he may not have, but I sure would have. I always listen to your advice."

Soon they were in the front porch, and getting rid of the wet clothes, to be washed, and hung up, by their Mother, at a later date. She looked unsympathetic to their arguing cause at all, other than the fact that they were cold, and some natural motherly love still shone through. Her presence moderated their tempers, and excitement, as always. It was one thing to be argumentative imps out there by themselves, and yet another in the presence of Mother. The argument abated. She prepared them each some hot cocoa and she lovingly warmed up some bread, with peanut butter.

They settled in, like cats on a warm day. The peace of the house, with the parental stability, and controlling of the conversation back to the fun part of their sojourn, soon had the boisterous pair looking ready for a nap. This was aided by the fact they had just run a five-mile race, and paddled hard on the canoe for an hour before that. The whole day's work had been on less sleep than normal, from the excitement of knowing a wonderful adventure was to occur. Emotionally, the adventure seemed over. The once warring duo relaxed together on the couch, only hoping that they could stay awake long enough to see <u>Bonanza</u>. Lazyhead's head started sagging into the pillow and Flipper's once anxious face had cleared itself of any conspicuous signs of anger. A nap, then supper, then sleep. Things were looking up. Life was pretty good, now that the petty argument was behind them.

When they were finally 100% cured, and relaxed, Father, with a definitely hesitant tone, put it back onto them. "So what about the canoe? Do you guys have a plan for retrieving it? Gotta do it today, you know. School tomorrow. I sure the heck am not going walking down through those bushes to retrieve it."

The Power of Clams

Ned, somewhere in his youth, had learned, or decided, to dislike English. It was not the English itself, but rather the power that another human had to decide on the topics of which to read, and to write. Besides that, evaluation of writing seemed horridly subjective. It seemed that if you had long hair, or a moustache, or expressed an opinion different than the teacher's, you were labelled 'dumb' for the duration of the course. You were destined to only maybe receive a passing grade, even if you hired a University professor, or your older sister to do the assignments for you. Ned had spent too many hours on the banks of the Battle daydreaming, and inventing unheard-of species of fish. This free spirit in him caused him to hold disdain for being told what to do. That power which teachers held to determine a student's thinking topic for the day, and even worse, his overall fate, fell forcibly into the space in his mind labelled 'resentment'.

This assignment was no different. The English teacher had handed it out for Ned and classmates to read:

Writing Assignment #9

The student is expected to compose an essay of no less than 1000 words, from a title of no more than 4 letters. Choose any four-letter word from the list below, or choose one of your own, provided it is apropriate within the school context.

Suggested title words: fire, work, tire, mind, word, tool, wars, soul, love, and soft.

The assignment is due at the end of this 80 minute class, and the purpose is to demonstrate that a writer can pursue detail, without loss of significant thought. Marks will be given more liberally to those writers that can relate these topics to historical or human significance, or use description, within the essay, employing clear expressive methods. Please avoid repeating or regurgitating the same theme within your work.

There was silence in the classroom, as students read, and then reflected on the assignment. Underneath most, if not all of the breaths, was the infamous 'f' word, or its lesser mate, the 's' word, the group's collective reaction to the assignment. Ned, and the other males especially, wished that this could have been a university class where perhaps the professor would allow exploration of the illustrious four-letter word. Alas, this was simply high school, and the teacher had warned them of trying any vulgarity in the guise of art, by the phrasing 'appropriate within the school context'. That phrase dismissed several ideas that students at least thought would be more conducive to providing lofty undignified adolescent-inspired detail.

As was common in this scenario, Ned sat, and appeared to be doing nothing, while his mind raced onwards in the quest of an appropriate topic, in this case limited to a four-letter word. The fact that the teacher had misspelled 'appropriate' only furthered his tendency to rebel. However, it also had the benefit of charging him up, turning him into a writing dynamo. Often, in these circumstances, he purposefully imagined himself sitting on the banks of the Battle, a setting more likely to bring about intuitive or creative thoughts.

He shut his eyes, and travelled to his preferred spot on the rock, above the gurgling rapid. He fantasised looking out into the current. "Clam." It struck him like a swat from a horse's swishing tail. Immediately he began to formulate words:

Clam

A clam is a dangerous creature, an unassuming invertebrate, yet still capable of summoning Yama. There are multitudinous ways that I shall set about proving this actuality, for it behooves me to justify. In fact, by the time the examiner is finished absorbing knowledge from this dissertation, he or she may positively be having nightmares on the gist herein, waking in the midst of night, all clammy.

The first of the clam dangers I shall elucidate lies in philosophy, to philosophers. A famed anonymous philosopher states, "A clam is a clam. A human is a human." To a clam, the species below him are nonessential twerps, placed upon the planetoid by a God whose inspiration, or creative action, included some form of species hierarchy. To a human, the clam is in effect, naught more than an animated stone, of no use at all, in the same way that subordinate creatures to the clam are nonessential. But of course, somewhere beyond this planet, if only in the realms of imagination, there exists a species that is proportionately evolved beyond the human, as the human is beyond the clam. Therefore, once the vastness of God's hierarchy is acknowledged, we prone-to-philosophise humans become nearly as insignificant as the lowly clam, in the grand scheme of things. The danger in this philosophical postulation is that our own humanity is thus trivialised to the rank of only somewhat higher than clam, which brings about depression in even the grandest thinkers, leading the best of the existentialists one step closer to doing themselves in, beckoning curtains unto themselves. Of course, the act of suicide of we humans is always a travesty, regardless of

63

the source, unless of course, as a rock star may have insinuated, it does indeed relieve one from the calamity (clamity) of an earthly birth, and there is no further consequence than that of a dogly rebirth, or heated days in purgatory.

The second category of thinkers that fall close to the brink are the historians. In the days of yore, supposedly, the clam was a form of currency. Certainly in the popular comic strip <u>BC</u> it is portrayed as such, and as we all know the powerful influence of popular media, especially the comic strip, this simple supposition permeates our collective subconscious. (Perhaps more postulation would lead to the analogy that the comic strip is as dangerous as the clam, but that would be another dissertation. For now we are limited to elucidating the evil of clams.) Personally, I find this, the idea that clams were currency, to be historical supposition at its lowest form. For I have amassed clams myself, of the freshwater Alberta variety. If the historical position is indeed undistorted, then we can equally assume that man of that era did not have an olfactory sense at all, which is highly unlikely under Darwinian ideas regarding rates of evolution. For the verity of the matter is that when a clam is kept out of its natural habitat, water, for even a few short hours, it commences to reek of its own rot. It gradually becomes a sickeningly vile creature, at least to the smellers of we humans, so much so that no sane and aware person would approach, let alone utilise the life-form as a primitive form of cash. The danger here is that with the reckoning of this minor historical misrepresentation appears the thought that perhaps all of history is equally false. Now this realisation too is a depressing one, but not an original one, and leads us to doubt the validity of any history at all. Hence we have historians joining philosophers in the hospital wards of depression, which poses another danger. It is clear we can survive without the philosophers, but without the historians, we would have no history.

A third critical danger lies to those among us who assure our welfare by predicting the ebbs and flows of value, the wretched economists, the pundits of cash. Let us assume for the moment, and for the sake of argument, that the historical suppositioner alluded to above, the rewriter of history, whom I claimed to be patently false, that he was actually right. Let us suppose that his supposition re use of clams as currency was indeed correct. It is indeed possible that our olfactory sense has evolved out of its precursor, nothingness. This then leads directly to this literary abuse of the economist.

The cause of their doom is very similar to that of the historian, for the roots of their demise lie in history. The same history that surmised the existence of the clam as coinage also surmised the first incidents of hyperinflation, counterfeiting, and black market economies. Today, these three economic problems alone, pose enormous threats to our structured society. The economist, poor fellow, by the selection of economy as his study, becomes morally obliged to thwart such economic threats, by proposing solutions. Today's economist has failed to learn from history. The historical era of clamism fell apart due to hyperinflation, counterfeiting, and black marketing.

Scoundrels soon discovered that currency was readily available in far off lands under the mud, and collected shiploads of cash, throwing the then economic stability of clamism into comprehensive and utter disarray. Today we label this hyperinflation. Have we not learned from our clam lessons? Poor Brazilians of today, amongst others, use wheelbarrows to move their cash about. Where were the economists, to allow this to happen?

Other cheats from the bygone era of clamism discovered that other breeds of clams than those meant for currency could be substituted. Hence they invented counterfeiting. Today, counterfeiting still poses a major threat to the financial management of a country. Although the government claims their branches of law and order have the situation in hand, any developed intellect, especially now, with the aid of computer technology, recognises that counterfeiting must have a significant impact on a country's economy. It is nigh time to abolish cash, but of course this would not be viable, for the corrupt government members themselves are no doubt enhancing their own pockets with the false stuff. Besides, are not they the delinquents that have the access to the authentic thing, giving them the advantage for higher quality copying? I've regularly pondered why the politicians seem to have deep pockets of cash at their inaugural speech parties. Perhaps herein lies the impetus.

Now I shall address the issue of black marketing. In clamism, the clam itself was replaced. Once the commoners saw through the corruption that had been brought on by the clam's use by the royals and merchants, they reverted to bartering, a much more sagacious approach to providing oneself with a living, to the dismay of the tradesmen and politicians of the day. History repeats itself. Current estimates throughout North American and European economies have suggested 30% or higher of the economy is underground. This is an enormous problem, for society to maintain order it needs government, a concept which in turn needs cash, from that cow we label tax, to survive. If the proportion of economy that is underground increases much further, it shall lead to the collapse of society as we fathom it. And this is all because of the clam. If God had not put that particular handy-to-grab species on the planet, perhaps all of these human errors such as development of currency, and sordid destructive mind-flows such as greed, would not have evolved.

So our compilation of occupations threatened by the clam grows. Economists are added to the collection, which already contains philosophers, and historians. Soon the asylums will be filled to the brim.

Next up are the warriors. Not many people know this, but once spelled out, it is patently obvious fact. The clam was the inaugural airborne arm to evolve, the first step upward from the stone. Old savages launched rocks at their attackers, and prey. But upon one historically auspicious day, when the fighting or hunting had coincidentally happened on a clam infested seashore, a caveman rather by mischance discovered that a clam is more suitable than a rock to impose wounds on the adversary, or breathing food source. The clam has a pair of simple advantages in comparison to a rock. The first is that the shape allows it to travel further through the air because of laws of aerodynamics. The second advantage is that its edge is sharp, meaning that it is more likely to inflict a cut, in contrary to the mere bruise of its predecessor, the menial rock. Cuts are significantly more damaging than bruises, for the innards are damaged as well, proven by the sight of a reddish liquid oozing from the infliction. In today's much evolved sport we call boxing, the match is even halted in the event of a cut, whilst bruises are simple outcomes that go with the sport, minor inconveniences for the athlete to work through, as are broken teeth in hockey games.

The fact of clams being weapons is further proven by the observation that ancient man invented a superior larger smoother artificial clam, and called it a discus. In early warfare there were three main projectiles, the huge weighty ball, the discus, and the spear. All evolved from rocks or pointed sticks, and all are honoured in the Olympics of today. But there can be no argument regarding the harm that weapon evolution has done to the planet. We have come a long way since back in Clamtime. Other factors, such as the moral misuse of gunpowder, and later forms of harnessed energy including today's nuclear weapons, have indeed aided in the elaboration of weaponry. But where did this all commence? With the clam, of course. Had not the Almighty put the sharp edged natural discus fellow on the planet, man may not have been able to embark, let alone evolve, such a destructive energy ebb we call warfare.

One sumptuous day in the far-off future, perhaps we, as humans, shall be done with warfare forever. The most optimistic of topical prophets even go so far as to suggest that that is the true fate of humanity, in contrast to the soothsayers who predict a woeful Armageddon. However, there is a problem to overcome, far beyond the days when warfare will be mere history. If the optimist would-be-oracles are correct, it is also logical to assume there shall come a time when not only is warfare no longer history, but it is *forgotten* history, meaning that the species we call human is so serene, that warfare as a concept is extinct. As long as there are subtle hints around, such as clams, what is there to stop some other unknowing dimwit to pick up another clam, and begin the evolution of warfare process all over again? The long term settlement is for a placid Big Brother to somehow rid this blue sphere of clams entirely, perhaps by exporting them off to some faraway planet, ending the possibility that one can ever again inadvertently be selected as an arm propelled arm.

Soldiers, and all those vile adherents of warfare, are hence added to the catalogue of people that need to be aware of clams, and their inherent danger.

The subsequent category that should become more aware of our antagonist, (the tester should know to who, I refer by now) includes psychiatrists, psychologists, counsellors, teachers, and any other class of people whose job it is to induce communication in other members of our species. The ability to communicate is perhaps the most important human characteristic of all. Withdrawal by force, medical intervention, fate, or self-induced anxiety means a shrinkage in the very thing we term human. While a common anxiety attack or momentary grump is ample enough example, the disease of Alzheimers is the extreme illustration. The affliction is a forced dementia that brings about vegetative states in we humans. One might conjecture how such troubles could possibly be blamed or even related to the clam. Well, that, colleagues, is very elementary. The clam was the one who catalysed the idea of non-communication to a human in some distant long past epoch, back in Clamtime, if you will. Perhaps a cave woman was having some grunted altercation with her cave-keeper mate. Perchance they were feasting on clams at the time. She, being dissed at her mate, recognised something in the clam that was of benefit to her. She noticed how taut its sides were clenched, and through the intellectual act of simulation, pursed her lips together in a similar way, and invented 'clamming' up. Now we all cognise the destructiveness in this force. Reticence is adopted as the weapon of choice in marital disputes. It is the stress-bringer to a fatigued teacher or solicitous parent just attempting to ascertain the answer to, "What the heck is wrong?" from a student or child. When people clam up, it wreaks total havoc on any relationship. Counsellors, psychologists, and psychiatrists *require* communication from their patients, even to make a living. (Although I tend to think that some would still embrace the patient's billfold at the end of the consultation, even if the allotted time was spent in absolute soundlessness.)

Clamming up, the observance, has been kept alive, not openly or consciously, but through the act of imitation of one's ancestors. It has been passed down from Clamtime to now. The only positive use for this emotional weaponry that I can dream of it is if somehow fricarious braggarts and politicians employed its use more often. Perhaps we could ascertain how to give them the malady, as in a means of germ warfare. If we could somehow deliberately cast it onto someone of our choice, I would not be so dejected. That could be like turning off that damn television contraption.

(The cursed clam is making me more and more hostile as I venture forward in this argument. I wish I could throw one off into the bushes, just to vent my accumulated fury from this writing, the reflective process that it is.)

The final argument is one that involves how our society has deteriorated into one of rabble-rousing and general partying. Societal behaviour has devolved into barroom brawls, murders, drug use, promiscuity, and miscellaneous sordid forms of sexuality, so much so that much of what goes on in the wee hours of darkness could hardly be considered human at all. Beasts of the night, we are referred to. Are there no morals left? Is there no harmony, no dictum? Are we destined to a society so depraved that the depravity itself alters society as we know it, to collapse inward, to the entrails of urbanity, as some black hole would pull the surplus of matter into itself, scrunching us all into some depraved screwed-up hallucinatory hell? Are we becoming victims of a plague of social chlamydia? And what the heck could clamhood have to do with this?

Why? Well, once again, my fellow compatriots, the explanation is indisputable. Somewhere in history, perchance on the shores of Newfoundland, Scotland, or the Caribbean, but more probable in that storied birthplace of western civilisation, Greece, a group of young uncivilised people visualised and then manifested their cognisance into a carousal called a clambake. Once having to do with the mastication of clam, the custom eventually progressed into a procedure of partying, a picnicking paradise, a spot to spout, a preliminary to the many plagues of mental restlessness that are commonplace today. Before clambake, there was placid peace on the planet. Now there is wanton waste, and only time will tell which path inhabitants of the planet will take: whether it will terminate in nothingness, or it will all come together into the much-desired utopia.

There are two more evident hazards of clams that I would be mistaken to not allude to. The premier is that they are sharp. You can ruin your flipper by treading on one. The second is that parents have a strange indoctrinated affinity for them and if a child should begin to entertain one, the clam sportsman should be aware of the dangers. There is a definitive possibility of an admirable scolding from the clam's human crony, the parent.

"Stop playing with those clams!" may be the unbidden obstreperous vociferation.

Life, it surfaces, is not so elementary as that anonymous philosopher's clam claim, "a clam is a clam, a human is a human". The simple may be dangerous, and the complex may be safe. Life is not so zebra black and white as such frivolous claims. For in this thesis, this exegesis, I have elucidated that indeed, given their historical significance, that a creature so unassuming as the almighty clam can, and did, impact our chronicles. This, without we so-called-intelligent creatures even having so much as a twinkling doubt that these mono-legged organisms may be menacing. Indeed, the peril is so much that we should tread far more prudently amongst them than one may have previously conjectured.

This had taken about an hour, and finally, Ned's head rose, his hand stiff from the enthusiastic writing. He looked around to see that some of his compatriots in English-hating hadn't written nearly so much as he. A sense of relief overcame him, and he strode confidently to the front of the room to hand in the essay. What mattered to him was that for once he had enjoyed this, and that he was going to get some sort of mark. He felt assured that he had written enough, and had gone into enough detail to warrant at least a passing grade from the teacher. Certainly it was worthy of a clammy 'C'. He did not concern himself with marks, although he did hope to pass. He realised that if it were not for those childhood days of idleness on the shores of the Battle, this event may well have yielded a different outcome, such as an empty paper, and the 'Zero' that it seemed the teacher would have enjoyed placing on it.

As he motored home that night, and across the river of his youth, he slowed, to acknowledge, in a humble way, both the river and the one legged simple fellow that dwelled in the mud sediment below the bridge, the simple catalyst that had MADE HIS DAY.

* To those readers accustomed to this author and publisher's mandate of an 'easy reading vocabulary level', please accept the writer's humble apologies. Fortunately for you, this is the only story like it, out of the 16 in this book.

* For you pompous asses who enjoyed Ned's essay not for its wit, but for its high vocabulary, I wish you the best of luck in obtaining your next better thesaurus.

The Purple Rose of Texas

Nancy loved those pokey strolls and meandering going nowhere drives with Grandpa. It was a unique time. He was gentle, amusing, and insightful, and a menace to anyone attempting to determine his truthfulness. They were quite the couple, she a questioning smiling six years, and he a wizardy crafty 60 some. It was ambience, and pure fun. More often than not, being only six, she was suckered into the stories. Older wiser siblings and cousins less often fell victim to his lies.

The Battle was a favourite drive then walk spot. Down to the pastureland, where prairie wool and cacti grew abundantly on the plains and hills, and silver willow filled the draws. Lately, Grandpa, the prairie botanist, was in the act of teaching Nancy, who was an eager questioning student, the names of all these things. With Grandpa and the truth, there were three possibilities:

1) He knew the plant's name and told the truth.

2) He didn't know the plant's name, and made one up.

3) Or, the most common, he knew the name and still made up a new more romantic or sneaky name.

As he went to open the gate to the pasture, she saw a large pretty flower across the ditch, near the fence line. When he returned from the gate, her regular, "What's that, Grandpa?" followed, as she pointed.

Never one to be slow in responding, Grandpa started the illusion. His face lightened with enthusiasm, and his voice was of mild surprise. "Why, I haven't seen one of those in years! They're not very common around these parts. It's pretty, isn't it? Shall we go take a closer look?"

She was always ready to take a closer look, so she clambered out, and headed across the ditch.

"Don't touch the stem," he called. "It's a might prickly."

She heeded his call, and approached with caution to marvel at the deep purple blossom on the top. When he got across, she inquired as to a name, again.

"That plant's called the Purple Rose of Texas," he said, face straight as the crow flies, as with all his fibs.

"But it doesn't look like a rose, Grandpa?" She wasn't altogether convinced.

"Well, Honey, there are lots of roses. I guess the ones in Texas look a little different. But the reason you know it's a rose is because of those prickles on the stem." He pointed closer. She leaned over inquisitively. For sure there were lots of dangerous pointy things.

"I bet you've been scratched by a wild rose bush before, eh?" He was a skilled stringer.

"Yes, Grandpa, I sure have. Last week, in fact, when I was helping Mommy pick saskatoons."

The seed was planted. Nancy had learned the wondrous name of another new plant, as with a few more wondrous names she had heard before, but for the fun of it, no one bothered to straighten her out. It was cute. When she and Grandpa returned for lunch that morning, she proudly shared her new botanical knowledge with Mom. Grandpa winked at his daughter-in-law. Mom wasn't positive, but Nancy's description seemed to be of a Scotch thistle, perhaps a Canadian thistle. Mom held her tongue to allow the myth to continue, at least for a while.

A few days later, when the flower naming pair arrived home with one for the vase on the kitchen table, Mom's suspicions re 'Scotch' were confirmed. "Look, Mom, I brought you a Purple Rose of Texas, so you could see for yourself!" The lass was so proud, Mom didn't have the heart to tell her the truth.

September arrived, and Nancy moved on, to a fresh environment, a place

71

where truth would more often be told. Grade one. It didn't take terribly long for the Purple Rose myth to spread. About two weeks in, Miss Langley, the teacher, had taught her enthusiastic, eager batch of students a fun game called the 'flowers and the wind'. Two teams, one being the wind, and the other being the flowers, line up at opposite ends of the field, or gym. The flowers select a 'secret flower', and the winds try to guess what that flower is. As soon as the guess is correct, the winds get to chase the flowers back to their home. Anyone tagged becomes a wind for the next round. The winner is the last flower left, or the last to be caught. (Through some very strange circumstances, the game has somehow evolved today into 'What time is it, Mr. Wolf?')

It was Nancy's turn to select a name of a flower. She had anticipated this day for a while, and of course proposed "The Purple Rose of Texas" as the next flower. One of those bossy grade two kids blurted out. "That's not a real flower. You can only use real flowers."

Nancy was shocked, and dismayed at this direct affront to her knowledge, and acquired prairie wisdom. "Yes, it is. My Grandpa said so."

The bossy one raised her hand, beckoning Miss Langley over to resolve the dispute. The dear teacher listened to both sides intently. Then she determined the outcome by whose ego being shattered would do the most lasting harm, and by whose tears were flowing faster. In that part, Nancy was a puddle ahead. Teach also no doubt had visions of swatting some old goat of a Grandpa who had put her in this precarious spot, having to referee a silly dispute caused by some old codger's ridiculous but creative fibbing.

Nancy's begging eyes won the battle. The teacher made her judgement. "We'll allow the Purple Rose of Texas. Maybe it is a real flower. No one knows for sure." Nancy beamed delight, and grinned wider than the old geezer, Grandpa, had he been there himself. Hypothetically, of course, his grin may have been vanquished by the nasty stare of one Miss Langley.

That particular round was destroyed of course, as the poor winds had to give up, never being able to guess what the secret flower was, until Nancy proudly yelled to all the winds. "It's the Purple Rose of Texas!"

Epilogue - In the days that followed, the popularity of the rare, but beautiful, Purple Rose of Texas grew immensely, at least in name. Fortunately, the nomenclature died out eventually, becoming extinct, within a couple of years, having only existed in the minds of a few prairie people. Unless, somewhere, sometime, a similar seed was planted by another old fibbing teaser. One can assume that the species itself continues merrily along with its original less illustrious name.

Orville's Struggle

The foremost way to get what you want out of overworked fathers is to be sneaky-polite. This is the law of father/son relationships. Either that or ask your Mother.

"Dad, do you think it would be possible for you and me to go try fishing in the Battle River?" he asked, in sneaky-polite dialect.

"That would be pointless, Son. There are no fish in that river. It's too darn small."

"Well, some of the kids at school today said that they caught some last Sunday."

73

"Then those kids must be liars. I've lived around here quite a while, and I've never heard of no fish in that river."

"Why would they lie to me?"

"I don't know. Maybe you lie to them. Maybe they just like to brag about things. They should have been in church on Sunday."

"But you know they don't go to church."

"Doesn't matter. Fishing is a waste of time, anyway."

That was enough. He wanted to say that 'church is a waste of time' but thought the better of it. No point getting it going with Dad. Dad always won, and sometimes Dad's winning hurt.

Well, sneaky-polite doesn't always work, but it was always worth a shot. Father wasn't much in the way of assisting Orville's curiousity about fish. Clearly this conversation was going nowhere. But those other kids most likely didn't lie, and he knew it. There was only one thing to do. Put plan two into action. If Dad wouldn't take him to fish in the river, at least he could go to the teeny tributary of the river, which was within meandering distance, and something he could do on his own. He didn't need Dad.

"Mom? I need some money for when we go to town. I need to buy some stuff." Orville was purposefully vague.

"What stuff, Dear?"

"I want to buy some books for school."

"You never read, Son." Mom was not to be duped just like that.

"Well, I want to start. And besides, I do so read. Just not the stuff they tell me to, though."

"That's what I meant, Dear." She looked at him, knowing that he was up to some harmless farm-boy stuff, and played along, as all good mothers do, without prying too far. The kid was only ten. "I know that you aren't telling the truth. Is this stuff you need dangerous in any way?"

"Nope." He was abrupt.

"How much money do you need, then?"

"About two dollars. Maybe less."

She reached for the purse. "Dad's taking a load of grain to town today, I think. Perhaps you could ride along with him, and pop downtown, while the grain is getting unloaded." She gave him two ones from the purse, along with that wholesome mother-smile that accompanied the giving of cash to young 'uns.

Mom was always easier than Dad. It was because she *understood*.

The hardware store had fishing equipment. The rods and reels were well out of his price range, but he'd known that before. Mom would have never forked over 15 bucks or more without him telling her exactly what he needed. All he wanted was some line and a couple of hooks. Where he was going there was no need for anything much else. Besides, these, he could hide in his pocket, and Dad wouldn't be accusing him of any stupid day-dreamy useless kid stuff like trapping and tree-houses, and bale forts. A boy's frolic was just fodder for Daddy's laying on of that functional wisdom. If it had no purpose, it had no point. Sometimes he thought Dad had never even had a childhood. He had just popped out of Grandma, driving a tractor, and forking hay.

The curious boy had no idea about hooks, and line, so asked the guy manning the store. "Mister, I want to do just a bit of fishing. What would you say I start out with?"

The sales guy pried a bit. "What kind of fishing, Son?"

Orville hadn't expected this question, and certainly didn't want to fess to this stranger that he was fishing in a place worse than McGelligot's Pool, a place where even the most optimistic of fishermen would disapprove. It was only slightly better than the horse-tank, or the ditch in spring. "Kind of like in a river, I guess," he mumbled, shyly, and with no force.

The sales guy pointed at the collection of spoons hanging on the wall. "Well, if you're fishing for jack, that red and white spoon there is as good as any. It looks simple, but it must work, because it's popular. We sell more of those than any other."

"Okay, I'll take one of those, and one of those plain ones over there, and also some fishing line, the cheapest kind you have."

After the purchase, Orville jammed it all into one of his front pant pockets, along beside the other regular stuff, like his jack-knife, his pocket watch, the battery, and the piece of petrified wood. The petrified wood was his awesomely auspicious good luck charm. The stone had replaced the real rabbit's foot after *it* had begun to decompose and stink. The petrified wood been there so long that he couldn't remember where he'd found it any more. Usually the pockets were so full that Dad would never notice anything additional, let alone pry. The only time he ever emptied them was at night to sleep, and when the kids at school begged him to empty them, just to see the collection. He could *almost* make money doing that.

He loped back to the grain elevator quickly, so that Dad wouldn't be held up, arriving just as the last remnants of grain were disappearing out the end of the truck. His father was occupied with the elevator agent, so he couldn't notice Orville's excited face.

Soon the pair had settled back into the truck for the long drive home. The driver looked at his young passenger. "So where did you go?"

Orville figured the chances of Dad even noticing he had gone off somewhere would be about 50-50, but just in case, he had an answer prepared. "I went to the other side of the elevator to watch for any trains going by. I walked down the track for a ways. That's all."

This was another valuable thing about hardworking Dads. They didn't have time to keep track of you, and formed the habit of not knowing what you were up to. At home it could go on for extended spells, like about six hours at a time, between dinner, and supper. If you played the game of keeping them thinking that you were with the other parent, or at least being checked on by the other parent, it was practically complete independence. Orville cherished that. It allowed him to do so much stuff that he wouldn't be able to do had they kept a better eye on him. Especially it allowed him to wander. He explored the coulee, entered a few old rundown deserted houses, and built play-forts in imaginary far-off lands. He was like a farm tomcat in his wanderings. Only his aims were self-created imaginary half-real adventures, not females. Those would come later, but at this prepubescent point, he had no idea about that stuff, fortunately for his parents.

When he arrived home, he snuck straight to his room, and retrieved the booty of the day from his pockets, and placed them on the chest with the mirror. He stared at the two hooks for a while, and imagined how they would look floating along in water. He would have to wait a week, until the next Saturday. Tomorrow was church day, and there was always too much family stuff in the afternoon. Then there was that week of that dreaded activity, school. He needed a lot more than an hour to go fishing at the creek, and the time between after school when he got home off the bus, and supper was about an hour. So the hooks and line would have to remain unused for a week. All those monstrous fish would subsist a while yet.

He moved the angling gear to his favourite secret cache at the back of his sock and underwear drawer, where even Mom never found anything. At least if she did, she never let him know.

Orville's home was about a mile away from one of the creeks that flows into the Battle, and from his place to the creek's mouth at the Battle was 10 kilometres as the crow flies, and about 50 kilometres or more as the creek wanders. He reasoned, after hearing there were fish in the Battle from those kids at school, that because the creek was connected, there might even be fish in it. It would have to be a dumb fish, but hey, Dad wasn't going to take him to the river, so it was either fish in this diphead creek, or not fish at all. Besides, from his rovings, he had learned of three or four beaver dams that held deeper water, up to three or four feet deep, at least. Probably more right beside the dam. So what if the creek was Lilliputian in stature. Besides, he had nothing to lose, except pride, should Dad ever find out. And he'd lost some of that before, with other failed dreams, so even being found out wasn't Armageddon. Dad didn't even think there were fish in the river, let alone the creek. But he had little to be concerned about. Many times he had gone off on his own without Dad even knowing he had gone. This little adventure was a piece of cake compared to the time he'd caught the neighbour's cat in a gopher trap he'd set in the wrong place. That little adventure hadn't gone over very well.

The only other thing that he had to do to ensure secrecy was listen for vehicles coming along, and then duck, and hide. This he had practised a lot. Dad wasn't the only adult in the neighbourhood that would think he was an idiot. In fact, most of his own brain thought he was an idiot. If it wasn't for his willingness to repeat the mantra, "I've got nothing to lose," he' wouldn't have initiated this darn project.

Saturdays never roll around quick enough to school-hating, restless boys. By Saturday noon he was nearly dead from the wretched curiousity/wanderlust. It was worse than having the measles. He gobbled down his dinner, and headed out, armed with the pockets full of jack-knife, the two hooks, the line, and of course, his petrified wood. It was all he needed to be Joe Successful Fisherman. His own enthusiasm was so compelling! Too bad nobody else could share in it, at least for now. When he brought back a fish, he'd be able to divulge his little secret to *them*. In fact he had the whole deal planned. All he needed was some co-operation from Mom Nature.

"That boy is up to something," he could hear his Dad say, as he hustled to throw on the gum rubbers in the porch.

The other necessity for his mutation into Joe Fisherman was a lengthy and straight willow stick. He was acquainted with the finest willow bushes in the valley, because he used willow to make bows, and arrows. A slightly bent green willow, with a length of binder twine, made a superior home made bow. The scrawnier newer growth around the edges of the willows, he used for those remarkable arrows of his, which could sail at least 100 feet in the general direction of his shooting them.

He headed for the coulee road, and once he got there, broke into a jog, which lasted straight through until he came to a decent willow patch, about half way down the hillside. Before entering the thicket, he stood still, and got his eye on the one that would become his own fishing pole. He spoke to the bush, as if it were a friend, "Please, Mrs. Willow," he beseeched, "let me borrow one of your straightest strongest pieces. It will be better off with me than with you. I shall treat it kindly." Once the decision was made, he got out the jack-knife, and with his acquired farm-boy strength, was able to cut it clean through on two cuts for the bottom, and one clean cut, for the top. Once back to the road, he turned and spoke again, "Thank you, Ma'am, for this young feller. You won't be disappointed." He resumed running, balancing the pole/friend alongside, and pointed it forward, parallel with the road.

He had pre-selected his destination: to the first big beaver dam just below the bridge. And if that one didn't have a fish in it, he would proceed another half mile downstream to the next one, and then the next. His pocket watch would let him know when to give up, and throw the pole away, and head back up home.

At the first dam, he found a patch of dry grass on the bank, and squatted down to hook up the rig. Being trained in knots from Boy Scouts didn't hurt. He cut a small wedge in the willow about an inch from the end, and wrapped the fishing line around it, and tied it. Then he estimated the distance from the top of the outstretched pole, plus enough for two feet into, and below the water's surface. At that point, he took the line to his mouth and bit through, as if he were a beaver. Then he knotted the line to the red and white. He stood, grabbed the low end, and held it up in the air, marvelling at his own creation. If there weren't any fish, at least he had a remarkable pole. That was something to remember.

He looked into the water, and imagined just where a fish might be laying in wait. The dam was about 5 metres across, and quite walkable. At most everywhere on the creek, except for dams, he could jump the darn thing. Certainly with the aid of a pole, and the horizontal pole vault method employed by creek-jumpers, he could clear it anywhere except right above this dam, or any other. He'd always wondered why the Olympics didn't have a horizontal pole vault event.

He spit on the hook for an auspicious boon, and whispered, "Okay, Mister, come out of your hiding spot." He reached out with the pole, and gently swayed it back and forth to cover the deep part of the dam, which he could do entirely without moving. After about a minute, maybe less, he realised that if there was a fish in there, it would have chomped the lure by now. The daydreams of endless hours whiling away the time on the banks of the creek, the way Twain portrayed boyhood calm on the Mississippi, was in fact, a huge mental distortion. This was no Mississippi, and he was no Huck Finn.

He whispered again, to the fish that wasn't. "Well, I guess, you aren't here. Hopefully, you'll be at the next dam."

He followed the bank so that his hook could remain on, and not stuck to any bushes. Where he remembered an obvious long switchback, he leapt across the spring to the other side. Soon he arrived at the second dam. He treaded carefully and stealthily to the centre of the dam, where he could once again fish the entire depth in one swoop of the pole. He told himself to pull the wretched red and white lousy spoon back and forth only a dozen times. He gave in after ten, which was entirely sufficient.

After the fifth dam, which was positively two tough miles from where he had initiated the transformation from boy goof into successful fisherman, his enthusiasm had dissipated entirely. He was still boy goof. Strung out, and fatigued, he sat on the last ledge, and shook his own head. "What a stupid fool I am, to think there might be a fish in this tiny creek! It's a darn good thing I kept my mouth shut. Dad will never let me off if he found out. I'm such a moron!"

Having sadly succumbed to the prospect of never ever catching anything but mosquitoes, rocks, or sticks, he decided to part with the two hooks and the line. "There's no point even taking you guys back up to the house. Dad's never taking me fishing anyway, and if Mom does spot these, she'll tell him, and he'll never quit bugging me til I die." He placed the pole, the hooks, and the rest of the line at the base of a straight but recognisable poplar.

"At least this way, I'll know where you guys are, if I ever need you," he whispered. They had become his friends, but now they had failed him, in his hour of need. He began the dreary trudge home, along the same route.

At the second to last beaver dam, he approached from the bottom side, and was watching the water bound out through the dam, in a foot high mini waterfall with those whispery splashes. As he advanced, it seemed to him that the water was moving in peculiar patterns, so he strode to the middle of the creek, which was nowhere near the top of his gum rubbers, and approached, half hoping it was a muskrat, or something. When he neared enough to see, his heart started pounding, as it was indeed a fish causing the oscillations. The sticks in the low edge of the dam had somehow formed into a natural trap, and in his efforts to go anywhere upstream, the stupid pike had wedged itself into the natural enclosure. Another few weeks of lowering water levels would have meant a slow sad death by drying.

Orville stood directly behind the trapped animal, and reached down into the enclosure with both hands, moved a sturdy stick with his left hand, and squeezed the back of the fish with the other. He grasped the slippery entity tightly, and wiggled it free, then tossed it up onto the grassy shore. It flopped around in foolish fish ways, as if it half expected to escape. There was no way. Orville saw to it. The poor thing was at least saved from the slower death from drying method, when he whacked it on the head to put it out of its flopping anguish.

Transformation from dreamer into real angler now complete, he hurried back to retrieve his hooks, pole, and line, so he could distort the story into one that he could be more proud of, for his Dad, up on the hill.

The odd, yet successful event gave him a second wind, as though he were a marathoner passing the last checkpoint. Fatigue vanished, and enthusiasm returned with gusto. There were indeed fish in the Battle. There were even fish in this ridiculous diminutive creek. Those kids weren't lying. He was right! Papa would pay.

Despite the arduous day, the run up the hill seemed shorter than the run down, for the first time in his illustrious wandering career. He imagined Dad's surprised look, and figured now for sure that they would find time for some real fishing. He had 1000 times the proof he needed.

He bounded into the kitchen, fish in hand. "Look what I caught! Look what I caught!" he yelled, as he held it high enough for all to see.

Dad looked up from the table, shocked expression and more. "Where in Sam Hell did you catch that?"

Orville's jaw opened too. It was the first time he had ever heard Dad swear. He glanced over at his Mother, who was equally in awe. "Down in the creek." Orville's only option was to tell the truth, even though it was absurd.

"Our creek?" asked Dad.

"Yep."

"But where did you get the hook?"

"In town."

"Where did you get the money?"

"From Mom." Orville looked over at his Mother, and immediately knew from her grin that she was on his side, if there was ever going to be a debate.

Dad continued the interrogation. "But just where did you catch the fish? That creek's practically dry!"

"In one of the beaver dams."

"What beaver dams?" Father still was having trouble believing his eyes.

"There are beaver dams on the creek, Dad."

Father paused this time, thinking he must be hallucinating, and shook his head to make sure. He stopped short of slapping himself. "Where in our creek? The thing is only a foot or so across some times. That's impossible."

"Nope. It was in one of the beaver dam ponds. About a mile downstream from the bridge on the road. Here is my fish. Do you want to touch it? It *is* real, you know. Maybe it swam up when the water was higher. Is it proof there must be fish in the Battle?"

Dad reluctantly gave it up, having obviously lost the argument, yet deeply amazed at the boy's accomplishment. He was quiet, humbled. "Yes, I guess it is, Son. Yes, I guess it is. Maybe some day we'll have to go down to the Battle."

Orville beamed. "That would be fun, Dad. Thanks."

The Initiation

Preface - There exists an urban myth that goes something like this: A pilot is on his very last flight before retirement, flying a Boeing 737 stubble-jumper jet, from Yellowknife to Edmonton. (or from somewhere to somewhere else) He turns on the sound system to have his friendly chat with the passengers, and explains to them that this is his last flight before retirement, and reminisces a bit about some of his more interesting passengers. Then, as he is closing his career-ending speech, he says, "But you know folks, these are powerful little jets, and there's one thing I've always wondered about them. And if there ever was an appropriate time, I guess this would be it. I've always in the back of my mind wondered what this baby could do, and we're about to find out. Fasten your seat-belts, please!"

What follows is a Battle River myth involving flight. Like most myths, this one has more than one version. The names and circumstances vary, but the ending is always the same. One of those versions is presented here. Like the foregoing urban myth, no one will ever know if it holds truth or not, but it's a darn remarkable game to imagine.

"Hi, I'm Warren." The man with the handlebar moustache reached out his hand. "I'm the fellow you spoke to."

"Hi. I'm Lee." The grade eleven student returned the friendliness, as their hands met. He felt a strange tad of deja vu, but rationalised it away to the excitement of the momentous event.

"Today, I'm just going to go for a flight, like I normally would if I was by myself. I'll explain things as I go along. It'll give you a sense of whether or not you actually want to do this. By the time we get back to the ground, you'll know." Warren, followed closely by the eager student, walked to the hangar door, and pulled it open. "The first thing we have to do is push it back out, and turn it around. Then I'll go through all the regular checks. All this stuff is routine and you have to do it every time you go up. There are those I hear, who don't, but it's always a good idea. I think they'd be morons."

Lee asked, "So you mean you always have to plan an extra half hour or so?"

"For sure. It's not like driving a car, where you just jump in, and start 'er up."

Lee was finally where his heart had been pulling him, at last. Ever since he could read, he had studied planes, and dreamt of this day. And this was only the dawning. He had pestered his parents for the last three years, on a twice-daily basis. His father had spoken to a banker about the potential for credit, to get him through some lessons, and to pay for the necessary flying hours he would require to get his pilot's license. When he'd read the ad in the local paper for: "A free introductory flight for those seriously interested in becoming pilots," he had taken it to Dad straight away. Dad had called Warren, the placer of the ad, and had found out the fine points. It was all quite informal.

Warren owned the plane, and went up regularly for his own indulgence. Usually he soared over the Battle Valley, scouting for deer, and just 'having a look-see'. He particularly enjoyed flying low, where there was more stuff to see, and you could see it better.

Although he had never taught flying, he figured he would, if the right kid came along, with the right money. The offering of a free introductory class was no huge deal. All it meant was that he would have company for one of his regular joyrides. Besides, if it was somebody completely naive and new to flying, it was fun to observe the fear, and excitement.

By listening to the callers, he could screen anyone who just wanted a free ride in an airplane. But if someone actually decided to learn, he would charge for the gas at least, and be able to pocket a little on the side. This personal joyriding became expensive after awhile. He reasoned quite soundly that there was a way in which he could have someone else pay for his adventures.

"You go to the front, and push, and I'll just steer from this end, and make sure the wing tips don't bump the doors." Lee ducked under the wing and moved around to the front. He was surprised at how light the plane felt, as he single-handedly shoved it out the hangar.

"Let's push it far enough so it can be turned around," Warren called out. Once the plane was a few yards out, he called again, while motioning with his arm in the air, "Now you go to the other wing tip, and you go that way, and I go this way. It's really easy to spin 'er around then."

Lee was still amazed at the ease of this. He hadn't realised how light a plane was. The leverage you got out at the wingtip made it seem even lighter. "This must be trickier by yourself, eh?"

Warren explained, "Well, not really. It's slower is all. Sometimes it doesn't back straight up. Sometimes I back it in, too. It just depends on my mood when I come in."

The pair connected at the front of the plane. Warren continued, "Basically, with the safety check, you just walk around it, once, checking everything as you go. Today I won't stop and explain everything, because that will take too long and you wouldn't remember it anyway. I'll lend you the book on this plane, and you can read up on it. That is, if after today you still want to continue. Have you ever been up before at all?"

"Nope. But I've sure dreamed about it a lot." Lee hoped that expressing his avid dreams would somehow impress the guy.

"Well, just so you know - not everyone takes to it naturally. Some people get really scared at first. A couple of times I've had to turn right around, and bring people back in, cause they were making such a fuss. One fellow even barfed on me."

"So where do you usually go?" Lee asked, curious as to what he might see that he'd never seen before. Certainly, whatever he saw was going to be from a much different viewpoint. The closest thing he had experienced to this new real perspective was staring dreamily at aerial photographs. Being naturally a confident fellow helped him to ignore any suggestions from Warren that he might get ill or be frightened. He could not imagine how anyone could fear that which they enjoy. He'd walked across high bridges such as the CNR train bridge, and had been in tall buildings, and recognised fearlessness regarding height, in himself, from those experiences.

Warren answered, "Usually I fly along the river valley. It's the best scenery around here, and it gives you a sense of height at lower levels, because of all the hills. We'll go up quite high as well. It's amazing how far you can see. That's neater at night, because on a clear night, you can see the lights of neighbouring towns, if you go high enough."

Warren led the eager youngster through the precautionary checks, and then opened the door to let his passenger in.

Lee climbed aboard. "It's much smaller in here than I thought it would be. I guess I imagined it more like a car."

"Yeah, that's pretty normal," agreed Warren. "At first you feel kind of cramped, but eventually you get really used to it. To me, it's almost, but not quite, the same as driving a car now."

As the pilot fired up the engine, he continued, "We have to let 'er warm up a bit at first. Then we're off."

Lee felt his stomach gurgle from the butterflies, as the humming began. Soon they were out on the grass strip, taxiing along to the far end.

The pilot shared his flight plan. "We're going to climb straight away, up to about 5000 feet. That will give you a good idea, of what it's like from higher up. Then we'll do a bit of cruising along the Battle Valley. I'll still explain everything as we go along, but you can feel free to just watch out the side window. If people ever have a problem, it's with the height itself, and the cornering. It can make you want to puke the first time. That's what the bag there is for." Warren pointed to the plastic bag in front of his passenger.

As they accelerated down the runway, and then lifted off, Lee was speechless. Warren had been right. The side view held his attention magnetically the whole while. They soared across the gravel farm road, and Warren kept it straight, as he had promised. When the little plane reached 5000 feet, he had it level off. He turned smiling to Lee. "Well?"

"That was fun. I don't feel sick at all. You sure can see well. I'm surprised at how everything is in squares so much, except for the valley. I'm glad I came."

However, as with all people, Warren was more than he appeared. This soaring thing he did not enjoy. It was just boring. That is why he could never have been a regular pilot. Regular pilots faced too many hours of the same thing. For him that wasn't exciting enough. Although he appeared to be a calm rather dull fellow, except for that moustache, inside he had a deep-rooted subconscious need, a need to impress. Never had he ever had any first timer up that he at least didn't put a bit of fear into. He watched for Lee to look away, out the side, and then reached over to turn the engine off.

There was a moment of odd silence, before Lee turned, "You killed the engine, didn't you?"

"Oh, no," he lied. "There's something wrong with it. We'll have to turn back just in case I can't get it going again." Warren initiated a long swooping turn, as the plane started descending. He thought to himself that either the youngster had heard from someone else that he played this joke, or he was just a cool not easily rattled kid.

Obviously, either way, the kid was not to be had. Lee complimented his new mentor on the ability to keep a straight face. "Ha. That's good. You look really serious."

It was equally obvious to Warren that he would have to proceed to step two.

"Sometimes in order to gain some speed in these situations, you have to descend quicker. The engine needs some speed to be able to start again." With this he proceeded to allow the plane to tip forward, and accelerate into a dive.

"Don't worry. Once we're up to speed, we'll pull up, and you'll be fine." He wished that he could frighten the boy.

"I'm fine now. What would make you think I'm not?"

"Usually people get a bit scared from this. Like they think we're going to crash or something."

"Well, that's not me, I guess." Lee was becoming slightly uneasy about this guy. Still he wanted to become a pilot, so he willed himself into at least putting up a front that he was not scared. He sat still, and felt the gravity increase as the pilot beside him pulled it even with the landscape about 100 feet above the ground, and turned the engine back on. Lee imagined the sensation was something like the bottom part of a roller coaster, perhaps somewhat better.

Turning off the engine hadn't worked. Neither had a forward acceleration into a dive, and pulling up at the last minute. With most people, that was enough. Sure, sometimes the key trick didn't work. But almost certainly the dive did. Warren was going to have to release his deviant, almost sadistic side. If you couldn't scare someone on their first flight, then you just weren't a real pilot. He'd learned this in the army, from the false (sometimes real) bravado that his comrades would go on about. Warren could only once remember having to go to step three. He and the buddies back in the forces had one evening sat around ranking various tricks on their apparent danger and fear-causing levels.

Warren inquired of the apparently cool young fellow beside him. "So would you like to feel what it's like to fly upside down?"

"Is that part of learning how to fly? Is that something that you're going to teach me?" Lee asked.

"Well, not really. Not unless you plan to join a stunt team. It's good though, to get a sense of all the different things that you can do," Warren coaxed.

"I don't really care. You're the teacher, and if you want to show me what that's like, I guess it's okay." Lee's suspicions were becoming reality. He had now concluded that this dude was willing to do whatever it took to scare the passenger, and in this case he was the victim. Then still he wasn't the type to just allow that to happen easy-like. He had wanted to be a pilot all his life and no one had given him any lessons on what was acceptable, and what wasn't within the parameter of the first flight. Not wanting to show the guy that he was frightened, even a hair, he went along.

Warren pulled a few levers, and soon Lee felt the tug on his belt, and the gravity pull to the roof. He looked out the window, and saw the earth above, the sky below. His stomach wanted to give in, but he feared that he wouldn't be able to control where the vomit went so swallowed hard to hold it in. After flying along inverted for a few seconds, Warren righted the two-seater, and looked over with a partially perverted grin.

"Well?" he beckoned again, for the response he wished. From the colour on the kid's face, it appeared that step three would resolve it.

Once again, to Warren's dismay, the kid sucked it up. "That was kind of fun. It was interesting to see the horizon from that angle. Kind of like standing on your head or riding one of those wild midway rides."

This comment only made Warren more resolved, on the inside. He thought back to step 4 in the army barracks chatter. He heard a comrade's voice in his head. "Stall and spin," it moaned, in a twisted deep tone. Warren could not remember the last time he had attempted the manoeuvre, but he knew it had been quite some time, as usually he was contented just cruising the valley, sighting deer. Apparently, if the voice inside his ego was correct, it was time to open the cache of trickery.

He looked over at his passenger, who appeared to be regaining some colour. "So do you want to see some more?"

Lee was unmoved, apparently. "Well, like I said before, if I'm gonna be a pilot, I might as well get used to some things. Whatever you want to show me is fine."

"Back when I was in the airforce, the one thing we used to enjoy doing was a stall, and then spin. Do you want to try that?" Warren wasn't so sure that he himself even wanted to try, but this kid seemed to be asking for it, so it was getting to the point of no return, ego wise. Secretly he wished the kid would just give in, and admit he was frightened a bit from the last one.

Lee answered somewhat nonchalantly, "Sure, I guess."

"Okay. It's been a while, but I think I still remember how to pull it out of the spin part."

The flight had progressed to a frightful situation. Warren doubted his own skill as a pilot, especially with tricky manoeuvres. Yet the kid was practically daring him to go on. He wondered where this thing was going to end. (The ego does strange, even preposterous things to certain insecure men.) It seemed to him, now that he had failed in three attempts at frightening the boy, that the only thing that he could do was bravely continue on. But where would this madness end? Would he have to crash the thing? Surely the passenger would at least puke at some point. Warren vowed to himself now that that would be enough. At least if the fellow didn't succumb to fear, heaves would do.

"What we have to do is climb, and keep climbing at a steeper, and steeper angle, until the engine doesn't have enough power to continue. This of course varies with the plane, but with this plane, because it's not really strong, it'll work. We'll allow it to power out, and slow down. Then the plane will start dropping backwards towards the ground, and that's when I have to let it turn to the side, dive, and then regain control. It's not as hard as it sounds."

Lee put on the courageous face. "Sounds like fun to me."

As the crazier by the minute pilot shot upwards into the sky, Lee braced himself for the top, and the transition into the sensation of falling backwards. Going straight up was relatively easy to stomach. He grimaced as he felt the plane slow down, and hesitate, then start dropping backwards. He noticed that Warren kept glancing over in his direction in hopes of seeing some fear, so he turned to pretend to look out the side window, and shut his eyes. This alleviated much of the nausea. His body was pulled forward in the harness, as if it wanted to be removed from the plane. He felt it decelerate into the backwards drop, and then turn to the side, and begin accelerating again into a dive, as they had done previously. He opened his eyes, to look straight ahead, but saw the earth spinning directly in front of him, so turned once again away from the pilot so he could shut his eyes without the pilot's knowledge. This was no longer very amusing.

Yet his will too, was not unlike the master's. As much as Warren wanted to make him frightened, he too was determined to never let on that he was. In the back of his mind, the thought remained that this guy might be his only gateway into pilothood. Indeed, perhaps all this stuff was par for the course. He wished he could recognise what was normal, and what was downright insane.

When the plane evened out again into horizontal, he intellectualised the experience. "You know, that trick was okay. Now I know what it feels like at the very top of a tossed object. In Physics 20 we learned that a ball, when thrown straight up has a moment when it actually stops, right at the top. I never thought I would feel that sensation. I'll have to talk to the Physics teacher about it on Monday at school. He'll probably have a lot to say."

Warren had had plenty. That was about the most nauseating manoeuvre he could think of for this plane. If he had a different plane, there were probably a few more he could do. But it seemed to him that this would have to be it. His solace came in the knowledge that he had done his best, under the circumstances. You simply cannot win them all. Had he been a bigger man, he'd admit it to the companion the real purpose for the stunting, but he couldn't bring himself to such a disgracing act. He turned and spoke, "I think we should just cruise the valley, and see what we can see."

"Is there much to see?" asked Lee, figuring that there wasn't much.

"The most interesting structure around is the train bridge south-west of Fabyan. We'll cruise on down to there if you like."

Lee jumped into the conversation quickly, hoping that the stunting was over. "That would be a destination, at least. My friends from town and I used to go out there when we were kids. It's a pretty neat place. We'd go out on top, and wait for a train to come. Then we'd stand on one of those safety side things while it passed. The whole thing shakes quite a bit, and the train whizzing past makes bit a bit windy."

Warren was beginning to realise why this lad wasn't easily frightened. It seemed that he'd been around more than just a tad in the realms of fear. "Well, let's go have a look, then."

On the way down the valley, looking out the window at the hillsides, Lee reflected to himself on the reasons why Warren had taken him on such a wild ride. He concluded, after the quieter reflection period, that there was only one real possible reason, and that was that the guy had actually been trying to shock him. Besides, he had allowed himself to get caught up in the moment, mostly because it was so thrilling. He wished he had more time to think in such situations, and wouldn't get caught up in momentary excitement or dares quite so easily. All too often people speak too soon, and regret it afterwards. All he really had to do back there was to say he was a bit scared, and surely the stuntman would have ceased his demented act. In fact, at the beginning of the flight Warren had even hinted that it was okay to come back in by telling Lee that others had gotten scared and he'd brought them back to land. Why couldn't he be more reasonable, and admit fear? He thought how fortunate it had been that Warren had discontinued on his own, after the stall and spin routine.

He peered ahead, and could see the bridge in the distance. It was a magnificent sight, for the prairies, spanning the whole valley, at least a mile long. He looked over at his pilot, and was overcome by a more powerful sense of deja vu, but couldn't put his finger on it. So he asked. "It seems to me, Warren, that I've seen you somewhere before, but I can't figure it out. It has something to do with the bridge, I think."

Warren paused for a moment, recalling his own day spent at the bridge, and wasn't sure if he wanted to get into it, out of fear of where the conversation could head. But the kid had asked, and he deserved some kind of answer, so he spoke. "I've only been out there on foot once. It was a few years ago."

Lee pried onward, still hoping to conclude his curiousity regarding the mystic feeling. "Oh. Were you fishing, or just looking at the bridge?"

"To tell you the truth, we were measuring the bridge." Poor son of a gun fell for it. The ego had regained its hold, and had begun manipulating common sense once again.

Lee's face lightened. "I think I remember now where I know you. We were there that same day, and you and another guy were underneath the bridge. You had a long tape measure that you threw across the river. You didn't have that moustache then, did you?"

"Nope. Like I said. It was quite some time ago."

"So what on earth were you measuring the bridge for?" Lee could not think of a single solitary reason.

Warren sighed, indicating an unwillingness to get into this, but the kid kept asking. "We wanted to know how far the span was right above the river."

"But what for?" The persistent little bugger pried on.

"We wanted to compare the span with the span of this plane." Warren looked at his passenger in disgust, from the kid's tenacity, and his own imbecility at not being able to avoid the topic altogether.

Finally the lights went on, bringing the curiousity seeker out of his stupor. His face lit. "Oh, I get it now! You and the other guy were thinking of flying *under*, weren't you?"

Warren nodded a resigned non-verbal, "Yeah, and you must think we were gawdawful foolish."

"So did you ever do it?" Lee was aroused beyond repair.

Warren distorted the story, as any good egoist would. "No. There was only about 3 feet on each side. The guy who was with me, Max, moved away, and I never got around to it. It wouldn't have been the same without him."

In actual fact the pair had come to their senses, and had realised that not only would it have been illegal, there was potential for wanton waste of lives, and property. At the time Warren had been damn scared too. The span was just too close. They had gone to the extent of calculating how wide the plane's wingspan was if they went under it at an angle. That would have given them a few more feet on either side, but in the end, the whole sordid plan was doomed. Even if they were to have succeeded, there was a decent chance that someone may have observed them, and reported them to the authorities. It was also likely that Max would have been unable to shut the heck up about it, braggart that he was. Max had moved away though. At least he wasn't lying about *that*.

Lee saw his chance at revenge, for those aeronautic stunts he had been forced to endure. It was instinct, not thinking, that made him think of it. "So were you frightened?"

Warren's response was downright shameful for its lie, "Oh no. I wasn't scared at all. Max was pretty scared. I just didn't do it, because he wasn't with me. Those things are just more fun with two people."

"Well, today there are two of us," Lee proposed.

This was precisely what Warren didn't want to hear. The last thing in the world he wanted to do was to fly through that hole under the bridge. Back when he and Max had explored the possibility, he was more of a risk taker. Since then, his life had stabilised a whole lot, and doing something so idiotic, so semi-suicidal was downright nuts. If it weren't for that dang pride of his! "Well, I suppose that's true. We'll have to take a look first though. There will have to be no people on, or anywhere close to the bridge. It has to be that no one sees us. If word ever got out I did a stunt like that, I'd lose my pilot's license for sure, and then where would you be? You would no longer have a teacher." He tried to put some blame for this ordeal, on his student-to-be. If the small plane would have had a kneeling bench for prayer, Warren would have knelt, praying that some people would show up right about now, somewhere close to the bridge. He needed a decent excuse.

Lee was commencing to enjoy the old boy squirming, and he thought that it was just about fair, seeing that he had been put through some fairly decently wicked aerodynamics a few minutes earlier. "Well, fly by then, nice and low, and we'll look for people. And if there aren't any, you can show me how brave you are. I think it would be a hoot to go under the bridge."

Warren flew south along the east side of the valley, so that his passenger could have a good look, praying for a person sighting somewhere. After having passed the bridge he queried, hopefully. "So is there anyone close by?"

Lee grinned. "Nope, not a soul. I guess you're going to have to do it, eh?"

Poor fellow had two losing choices. Either he had to do it, as Lee had said, or he'd have to admit defeat in the fear/ego battle. He, the experienced pilot, admit defeat to a mere beginner?

Nope. He turned once more at the passenger, and stared. "Okay, then. Hang on!" The moronic ego-induced fool went for it. A dare is a dare. A true daredevil never refuses one, just as a true Irishman cannot refuse a pint o' Guinness.

He brought the small plane down close to the river itself, using it as a visual guide to where he'd have to end up. Then he looked forward from the cockpit, and aimed the plane for the very centre of the opening underneath the million-dollar structure. Before he realised the full stupidity of the thing, it was too late. He didn't have the time to lift up, and soar over. On the approach, he braced for the impending collision, but kept his eyes open for the aim.

What remains is the sacred secret flying myth of the Battle Bridge. According to it, the pilot fellow Warren, having succumbed to the young man's dare and to the power of his own egotistical nature, made an elegant pass beneath the bridge, angling the pint-size plane perfectly so that it cleared, roughly equal on both sides.

As the plane cleared, the pilot let out a gentle "Wow!" It was more one of relief than victory.

Lee looked over, and felt suddenly extremely uncomfortable. He hadn't realised exactly how dangerous the stunt was until he saw how close the wingtip was to concrete, and looked over to see the colour on Warren's face as they cleared. Near-death experiences, especially those from your own risk taking pride-induced stupidity, should, and do bring on grey clouds of discomfort. It's like going to the funeral that could have been.

As soon as the plane came out the other side, Warren lifted back up, into a quick straight path back to the airstrip.

To this day, for fear of being brought to task for the dangerous stunt, he and passenger Lee have kept their vow of secrecy. Unless of course a listener-friend should get either one rummed up sufficiently enough to have his tongue loosened. Then it's the whole sordid adventure over again, for the benefit of some admiring young daredevils.

* Regarding the myth - If you ask the right guy in the right town... Well, who knows? Perhaps *you* could be taken for a ride.

Why Frosty Stopped

Publisher's Note

This story contains reference regarding the use of an illegal drug, in particular, LSD. The publisher and author wish to clarify that in no circumstance do we condone the recreational use of such drugs. This reference is in the story to more accurately portray the characters, or history of the time, which was the late 60s or early 70s.

*   *   *   *   *

There is nothing so quite like the mystical mind expander of the 60s, lysergic diethylamide, to provoke questioning or intense imagination in the minds of men, or boys, or girls, as it were.

"Why can't I just step outside and disappear?" Toast questioned.

"No reason, really, I suppose," Leaper replied, optimistically, as if he hoped it would actually happen, for shock value. At least it would be a tale to tell the grandchildren one day.

Leaper imagined his future, "Well, you see, Son, back in 1969, there was this magical drug, called LSD for short, that had these miraculous qualities, and one night a bunch of us were sitting around when my friend Toast simply walked outside, and disappeared...vanished... into thin air!'"

Perhaps if Leaper's friend did disappear, it would end this philosophical debate, at least momentarily, or until the next serious acid trip. Music might be a more welcoming topic, more inclusive to everyone there, not just those acidhead ninnies who were prone to questioning the very existence of themselves, of God, of the chairs they sat on, of matter, and whatever else gripped their drug-impaired collective attentions.

In the late 60s, acid was king, and yes, even in certain naive rural towns around the Battle. Now this wasn't San Francisco's Haight-Ashbury district, but still, children love to pretend. If you couldn't afford a real trip to hippydom, at least you could buy a Doors record, drop some LSD, and *experience* the dream.

Drop out, live off the land, and Steal This Book were the orders of the day, for some. Toast, Leaper, and friends followed those orders by indulging in the hallucinogen, secretly of course, beyond the grips of conformity, of school, and of law.

"What factors would make it more possible?" Toast continued, unaware no one was paying attention.

"What?" asked Leaper, who had momentarily become attached to the music.

"To disappear."

"You're still on about that, eh? Well, I think that perhaps it would be easier on a very cold night."

"Why?" Toast wondered. Perhaps Leaper was on to something.

"Why not?" Leaper proposed the everytime answer to the 'Why?' the big reoccurring question, on acid. It always worked, yet never worked, this 'Why not?' "Perhaps the molecules are travelling slower when it's cold, and the other side could just pick them up easier, because they're travelling so slow, you know."

"Makes sense," agreed Toast. "Then again, if it was hot, the molecules would have more energy, would be travelling faster, and therefore, would be more likely to burst through to the other side, eh?"

"I suppose. Either way, your chances of it actually happening would be increased. Somehow I don't think it's going to happen tonight. Besides, who is to say that the other side even exists? Just cause Morrison sings about it, and some old stories, like that one about the lion have it in them, doesn't mean it's true."

BB, who had been listening in, but not quite ready to add his two bits to the philosophy, suddenly jumped up from the sofa, a spot to which he had apparently become glued, until now. "Look," he half-yelled, "if you want to disappear, just go for it. Don't just sit around and talk about it. Walk outside and disappear, if you like. There's the door." He pointed to it, and motioned for the pair to head there, as if this ordinary house door was suddenly transformed into *The Door*, to the other side, to Narnia. Perhaps, better yet, it was the door labelled 'For Madmen Only' from Hesse's Steppenwolf.

Toast and Leaper looked at each other as only boys on acid can, in the moment, and in the realisation that BB's notion was correct in its assertion of putting words into action. For to talk is one thing, but to *experience* much more, indeed.

"Let's go, then." Toast stood, and beckoned his friend to join in, to enter the ether, to go over to the 'other side', beyond the beckoning door.

"Put on some Doors," said BB, over in the general direction of the stereo, but nobody heard, everyone being so tied up in conversation or other fixations. "It would be appropriate." He turned to Toast and Leaper. "I bet you guys come back," he said. But they didn't hear, so absorbed they were in the prospects of their disappearing act.

So out the stoned pair went, together, as if joined in mystical travelling into the other dimensions, space travellers hopping about from one galaxy to the next. They stepped outside, beyond the real door, and walked around the corner of the house, into the moonlight, and cold of the harsh Alberta winter.

"You go first," said Toast, and motioned for his pal to head off towards some trees, in the general direction of a wondrous display of aurora borealis, a sure sign of a mystical calling.

"Okay, but you promise you're coming along, right?" Leaper spoke with trepidation. Should this vanishing event really happen, he did not wish to go it in isolation.

Toast grabbed his friend's arm. "Look, Buddy, if you actually walk over there, and depart, I will for sure join you."

"Okay, then. I guess I'll be seeing you around, one way or another." Leaper took a couple of hesitant steps north-east, toward the aurora. Then he stopped, frozen momentarily, in time and space, imagining his body, disappearing, and phasing into the nothingness, of the other side. He stood motionless for what to him seemed like forever, but which was actually only a couple of seconds. Reality and the hallucination were nowhere near close, in the drug-distorted concept of time.

Toast watched, as his friend stood, obviously attempting to will himself across. Or through. Or beyond. Toast didn't know if he would be *able* to follow. Perhaps his buddy had expertise that he himself didn't. Who knows?

Soon Leaper turned back, his face showing disappointment, in the failure to succeed at this. He retraced his steps, being careful to step backwards, as if he were a home video in reverse. "Well, I gave it my best shot," he asserted, "but I guess tonight just isn't the proper time and place. Maybe later. Do you want to try?"

"Not really," replied Toast. "If you couldn't do it, I positively doubt if I'll be able to."

"Hey, look at my tracks," observed Leaper. "They just stop suddenly, over there. Someone might mistake it for someone actually disappearing, the way it looks."

"You're right," agreed Toast, "but somehow I don't think anyone cares. When you gaze up at the sky, we both seem so irrelevant. So trivial. So insignificant."

Together they returned back inside the house. No one noticed as they re-entered the ordinary side, for all their friends either didn't care, or were still too busy with their own hallucinatory worlds. They sat down together on the couch.

Toast turned wonderingly. "I wonder how come it didn't work."

"I think it just wasn't risky enough," said Leaper. "I think the chances would be better if we were outside, alone, or out in the country. It's probably a bit like alien abductions. There's no way that those dudes would drop by here where there's this many people. All the stories you hear have people going down lonely back country roads, and disappearing. I've read about that, where the tracks in the snow just stop, cold. Of course, the cops and the authorities never file full reports on stuff like that. It's just too weird."

"Too weird," agreed Toast, now lost in Leaper's reply, it being too organised and lengthy for him to follow. "Hey, now that could mean a lot. Too weird. Lots of things are too weird."

"Right, man. Aliens. Disappearing. This whole party. Us. The weather. The acid. You're right. It's all too weird." Leaper was ready for a new topic.

"You know what's really weird," he continued. "School. That's what's really weird. I'm beginning to almost hate it. The whole darn place seems so stupid these days. Here we are, all stoned up, and having real philosophical discussions, and well, there in school, it's just so different. You aren't allowed to think somehow. I can't really explain it."

"I think I know what you mean. English is the worst. It seems like the teacher just wants everyone in the class to think the same way. If you want to get a fair mark, all you have to do is listen and agree. I think that's so stupid. You can't even write what you want to write. If you write about violence, or sex, or stuff that is the least bit off the norm, you get low marks. Too bad we can't cube (slang for 'placing a drug into') some of those teachers' coffees with a little acid. That might liven up school for a day or so, eh? Can you imagine writing about acid? The poor teacher wouldn't have a clue what we were talking about." Toast rambled cynically, and hopefully.

"So what did you think of that poem about the dude stopping his sleigh?" asked Leaper.

"Frankly, I didn't care. I just wanted to get out of English class so we could look at the girls' legs. If it weren't for that, I'd be totally bored. The poem was okay, but I sure didn't think it needed to be discussed for half a week. I wanted to just ask, 'Can't we move on to something else?' but I figured that would give me another little black mark in his book."

BB had been listening in again, and figured he'd put in his two bits, "Well I, for one, don't think the guy was contemplating suicide. I think that was just something the English teachers dreamed up so poor youth like us could waste more time sitting around thinking about it. Maybe it's an excuse to go into how futile suicide would be, an excuse for lecturing morality."

Toast laughed, "Ha. True enough. Too bad Frost, or whoever it was, couldn't just come here, and tell us what he was thinking. That would sort of be the reverse of disappearing. Reappearing. Than at least we'd get to the truth. Only the poet knows what the poet was thinking for sure."

Leaper nodded his agreement about the poet, but warned Toast. "Don't you go get started about disappearing again. That was stupid."

Suddenly Toast's brain shot back in time to a few minutes earlier when they had been outside. "You know what we should do? We should play a trick on someone who is really stoned, and tell them that one of us walked outside, and just disappeared, into nowhere. We can show them my tracks. Who should we pick on? Who's really gullible?" The three of them stared around the room to pick out an ideal fellow stoner to dupe.

"Sarah," said Leaper, emphatically, when his eyes settled on her.

"For sure." BB agreed, and Toast nodded.

Leaper's eyes lit up at the prospect of having some fun, and getting back outside where life under the stars seemed to hold more mystical richer qualities, than in here. His mind unfolded the plan. "BB, you go to the can. Make sure that she doesn't notice you. Then right away Toast and I will get her, and inform her of the story. We'll take her outside and tell her that we saw you just disappear, and show her the footprints in the snow. She'll believe it, I bet. Then, after about five minutes, we'll come back in, and you'll just be sitting here on the couch."

The three pranksters nodded their heads together, and BB headed for the can. Toast and Leaper watched him go, while maintaining an eye in Sarah's general direction. As soon as the washroom door closed, they jumped up, and headed in her direction, over by the stereo.

"Sarah? Got a minute?" Leaper looked at her.

"What's up?" she asked.

"You have to come with Toast and me for a minute." He grabbed her by the hand, and leaned over to yell in her ear, above the music, which was now some blaring Rolling Stones. "You'll have to come outside so we can explain it."

Leaper led her to the cold Alberta outside, and Toast followed.

As they closed the door, she correctly observed, "Jeez, it's so much quieter out here. You can actually hear yourself think. Kind of nice. So what's the problem?"

Leaper looked at her, seriously. "Well, earlier, the three of us, Toast, BB, and me were talking about how we read somewhere about people disappearing. You know, like tracks just stopping in the middle of nowhere."

"So?" Sarah was beginning to shiver, and wanted the story to go quicker.

"Well, we decided that rather than talking about it, we should just go outside and attempt it. I think it had something to do with the acid. Anyways, the three of us came out here, and BB agreed that he would journey first."

"So?" Sarah was shivering even more. "Just hurry up the story."

Toast piped up and pointed "Look over there at those tracks. We thought he was just fooling around."

Sarah's eye's widened as she observed the tracks closer. "You mean!..?"

"Yep." Toast cut in on her. "The guy just sort of melted away, and then he was gone. Now we don't know what to heck to do about it."

"Ahhhhhhhhhh!!" Sarah was caught right up in the dupe, from the dope. "So that's what this is about. What are we going to do about it? What will his parents think? Don't you think we should call the cops or something? This is really really scary." Her volume increased with each sentence.

Leaper calmly put his arm on her shoulder. "We were kind of hoping that BB would somehow be able to figure out how to come back, too. It sounds to reason that if he figured out how to cross, that at least he could likely figure out how to get back, too. He's a pretty resourceful fellow, you know. The worst part was that we told him we'd go too, if he made it. Then when we watched him disappear, we chickened out."

"Yeah, I guess. I woulda chickened out, too. Are you guys okay?" Sarah turned her concern to the survivors.

"Oh yeah. We're still here, aren't we?" Toast tried to reassure her. "Maybe later one of us will get the guts to try to follow him to wherever he went, and bring him back. I doubt very much if that guy will be me, though."

"I think we should go back inside to figure this out. Maybe someone else will have some ideas. Besides, I'm getting really cold." Sarah had had enough, and was looking pale.

She was the first to re-enter the house. The sofa was immediately inside, the first thing to see. There on the sofa sat BB. Sarah's face seemed to gain colour immediately. She went right up to BB. "Hey, you're back. How did you get back?" The dupe was amazingly alive and well, due to her being so stoned, coupled with her natural gullibility.

BB played the game, as he smiled beyond her caring face to the two rats standing behind her. "Oh it was really hard. The place was a huge empty room, like a ballroom, and it had this huge golden door, and I figured that it was either the entrance to heaven like in 'Stairway to Heaven' or it would allow me to just come back. I wasn't sure. I also thought it might lead to a stairwell going down, you know, like a strange welcoming from the Devil before he takes you in. Strange, I shut my eyes as I entered the door, and when I opened them, here I was, sitting on this couch here. Actually, I am extremely relieved. How did you know about it?"

"They told me," she confided, proud that it was she who they had asked to help. "Leaper and Toast."

"Oh. Well, I guess that's that. I'm not going back, though. Maybe next time I won't be able to come back here. Next time Toast is going to go."

"I'm just glad you're back." Sarah bent over and gave him a friendly hug before going back over by the stereo to restart her own adventures of the evening.

The duper trio sat and laughed, at the silliness of the whole affair.

"Now, this sure the heck beats English class, eh, guys?" said Leaper, looking around. "Who do you think we can fool next?"

So the party continued with its array of philosophical banter, jokes, music, and wholesome fun, at least in that era, of the late 60s. No booze. No fights. No sex. Just rebellion of the intellectual variety, aided along by an illegal drug. There was lots of discussion regarding disappearing, analysis of music, and of course disdain for the mental, psychological, and physical confines of school.

By three AM, the hallucinogen's effects had worn off, enough so, at least, that Toast was able to drive. Most of the party animals had only to walk home, but his trip was further. He had to drive some ten odd miles, over the Battle River, to home.

Alone in the car, his mind kept rushing, in circles, over the night's set of experiences. He really did wonder about the disappearing bit, whether or not indeed, if the right circumstance were to prevail, if he could in fact, disappear. He wondered about Leaper's supposition involving risk: that if the situation involved risk, that then the likelihood of vanishing actually happening would be increased exponentially.

It occurred to him that the ideal way to test this theory out would be to jump off the Battle Bridge, in the middle, down to the frozen river some 20 metres below. Surely, if one was able to vanish into another dimension, that would be a most suitable place. Certainly risk was there, and if Leaper *was* correct, it *would* surely happen before the body hit the ice. The thought was at once entertaining, and frightening.

As the car approached the bridge, his mind flip-flopped between speeding up, or stopping. He was afraid that if he stopped, and decided to jump, that if it didn't work, the event would simply become one of those jumping off the building stories he had heard about regarding the dangers of LSD, from teachers, and anti-drug campaigners. On the other hand, it was an interesting concept: the bridge was quiet, and he would be alone, completely. The aurora borealis was still flaming and dancing beautifully. If he turned the car off, there would be a wonderful stillness there.

In an insightful flash, he realised his actions were paralleling those of the poet's. It was a snowy evening, he was alone, and he was in a contemplative

97

mood regarding two paths. There were minor differences, such as he was stopping on a bridge, instead of just by woods, and he was driving a car, instead of a sled. But in the grand scheme, these were minor, and could be written off by the fact he was in a different time, and place. He felt that it was possible he was Frost reincarnated.

He stopped the car at the side of the bridge, judging the very middle of it, turned the engine off, and got out. Indeed it was extremely quiet. He could hear nothing at all. No leaves were rustling, as it was the dead of winter. No engines were purring, as he was at least five miles away from the nearest house. The light windless snow deadened the sound even further. All this gave him the thought that positively, if there were to be an alien abduction, or if he could exit this plane, now would indeed be the time and place. Toast looked both ways, in the silence, then advanced cautiously across the highway to the opposite edge of the bridge, to the precipice, to have a look toward the ice below. His natural fear of height did not hurry his advances much. Slowly, cautiously, he leaned over, hoping for some signal to beckon him on. But alas, there were none. No mystical calls beckoned. No beacons of light or humming sounds indicated the presence of alien forms. Only the last few remnants of the hallucinogen in his brain allowed such possibilities. Were it not for that, he wouldn't have stopped at all.

As he was leaning, the car's hood made a sharp twang, from the quick contraction of metal in the frigid air. He recognised it as more parallels to Frost. The car was beckoning, as Frost's horse had beckoned him. "Come on, will you? Just hurry up." Frost had returned, and moved on. Perhaps he should, too.

After a few moments of indecision, he turned back toward the car, somewhat disappointed, yet relieved. Apparently God, by not giving him any signs, wished him to continue the sojourn on this plane. No sign was the sign.

He went to the rear of the car, to relieve his bladder from the water and pop he had consumed at the party. A portion of the snow melted, turning yellow, and he wondered if somehow the snowfall would continue long enough to cover it by dawn. Perhaps people who drove by the next morning would notice and wonder who the moron was who stopped there to give his lizard a breath of fresh air. He hoped for additional snow.

As he zipped up his fly, and returned to the car to head home, another flash of insight rushed upon him, causing him to hesitate. The parallels to Frost now were extremely obvious, and he truly understood the poem, in only ways a mystic would comprehend. It had a whole lot to do with the pile of yellow snow, and very little to do with suicidal thoughts. Somehow he didn't think the English teacher would quite understand.

"The bridge was lovely, the river was deep,
"But I have promises to keep,
"And hours to go before I sleep,
And hours to go before I sleep."

* In memory of the wondrous nicknames of the era:

Leaper - The boy had a habit of leaping across campfires at bush parties.

BB - He went to a BB King concert with his older sister, and played BB's air guitar (Air Lucille) far too much for his own good.

Toast - His Mother's name was Melba.

The Salmon Run

There are no salmon in the Battle. Any biologist would know that. Any local, too. Still, all fish spawn somewhere. Even pointless pike must spawn. Pike cannot compare to salmon in any way. Lethargic, stupid, repulsive, and scaly, these Battle inhabitants are alluring mostly only to writers, as it is joyous to describe such inferior species. It's a whole lot better, and safer than referring to other humans, in such uncomplimentary ways, at least. Fish cannot file for divorce, or respond with closed fists, or well-aimed rocks. They take more kindly (or at least do not retaliate) to attacks upon the head, or on their purpose in life.

There is a legend, indeed it is more than that, it is part truth, that pike in inordinate numbers spawn in flats along the Ribstone Creek, in the spring. Many a local of that area knows about this legend, or tale, or fact, and many claim to have witnessed it. Not only on the Ribstone goes the myth, but on several other small creeks of the Battle, as well. Movies have been made about the elegance of the salmon spawn, how they endure severe hardship in the way of waterfalls and rapids, to return home, through some magical genetic knowledge. The pike is no salmon. Yet again, he cannot be as dumb as lore, for he (and she, presumably), do propagate the species.

The Ribstone is one of the few creeks on the lower Battle that used to have somewhat consistent water flow from year to year. Many of the smaller creeks dry up from time to time, and no self-respecting fish would have any genetic memory to head for that spot, where it had dried up. In fact, successful spawning could lead to a stunning dry death for the offspring, once hatched, should the adults ever return to the same area, encoded with genetic memory, as the salmon are said to do. Runoff rainwater tends to be less consistent than glacial melt.

(This author knows very little of the truth regarding fish of the Battle. As stated in the introduction of this book, they have never been studied much, and the Battle is so darned inconsistent from year to year. I suspect that some years there are great spawns, while other years, the spawn is non-existent. This is evident in walleye, particularly, as usually when a fisherman catches more than one walleye, they are identical in size, leading one to suspect they were hatched on the same year. Either that or walleye don't grow very fast.

Walleye to nine pounds and pike to at least twelve have been caught in the Battle. This fact is rather amazing, given the size of the river. It says something for the durability of the species as well.)

Thudder and Mac were just ordinary high school kids when they first discussed the spawning legend. Thudder's Mom had lived in the Ribstone area, and had told it to Thudder, when he was a young lad. For years, he had wished to investigate. The story goes that the fish get slow, and disperse in shallow muskeggy like areas, where they spawn. He had never been able to figure out if the legend held truth at all, as it wasn't beyond his mother to string him along. On the other hand, the story had sounded reasonable. The spot, and he wasn't even sure where it was, was some thirty miles from town, and high school.

When Thudder was younger, even though each spring he became curious, there was no suitable means of exploring. Asking his busy parents to take him out there was an unreasonable request. They had more responsible things to do. (Like work to support Thudder and his siblings)

Now, being in high school made Thudder's desires for answers a whole lot different. Mac, one of Thudder's many friends, owned his own car. Transition into carhood is a male's second most important transition, they say. For some, it is even the grandest. (Those become the guys who spend more time purchasing a car than selecting a mate.) The increased mobility that comes with the ownership of a car, or even friendship of a car owner, is dramatic. Suddenly the youth's world jumps from a couple of mile radius from home to about a hundred-mile radius from home. That's 50 times.

These guys were no geeky listless morons. Creativity in pranking, exploration, girl chasing, car manoeuvring, and general silliness, were their preferred pastimes. School was a place to partake in such activities, not the scholarly institution teachers and community leaders portrayed it as. Still, the pair knew the game of education, and played it well. Attendance was sufficient enough to allow for passing grades, and hence the future that the institution of education promised them.

However, if something more important should come up, such as the exploration of a childhood dream, or a sunny round of golf, or an afternoon of poolroom shenanigans, or a friend's invite to go water-skiing, an afternoon or two of no school presented few problems. Besides, these fellows were gifted with natural intelligence. (Times don't change much. These days, urbanite high school skippers find sitting at a dull mall watching old lady shoppers walk by to be far more of a learning atmosphere than school.)

"You know what, Mac?" Thudder said one day on the noon hour tour of Main Street.

"What?"

"There's something I've always wanted to do. It's a bit offbeat, but you know, I think we should just do it. This afternoon."

"Get to the point." Mac suspected by now that they would be skipping for the afternoon. Usually Thudder's adventurous suggestions were well worth pursuing, and Mac was not one to miss any opportunity of skipping school. Thudder's brainstorm would not have to be much. The allure of the sun itself was probably sufficient.

Thudder began to explain. "Well, when I was a kid, Mom used to tell me about this time of year that jackfish spawn out on the Ribstone Creek. She said they get really dumb and slow, and you can catch them with your hands. I've always wondered if she was just bullshitting me, or if it's the truth."

"It would be a horrible thing if a kid like you went through your whole life wondering about something like that, wouldn't it? There is only one way to find out, I guess, then," responded Mac. "We'll just have to go for a drive. Do you have any idea specifically where she meant? I mean, that creek goes along for a long ways. We can hardly follow it for a hundred miles." There was no discussion at all of skipping school. That was a foregone conclusion. Any skipper's excuse at all sufficed, and this sounded better than most. Mac headed the beater out of town in the general direction of Ribstone Creek.

Thudder turned navigator. "I think I can remember the road she said it was on. One day when I was just a little kid, and we were driving out there, she said that 'that's the place where those fish spawn' and pointed to it. It was from some bridge."

Mac smiled, "There are several bridges out this way. Every darn road that crosses the Ribstone has a bridge on it. Some even have two or three because of the curves. We might be driving around all afternoon."

"So? Still better than school. Even if I don't get my questions answered. Even if we don't find any fish spawning, you and I can go back to school tomorrow and tell everyone we did, anyway. Some of those girls believe almost anything." Thudder knew he was right, at least in the supposition that some of the girls they hung out with were gullible.

Mac continued his questioning. "So if this fish story is true, why didn't people just go and collect a whole bunch of them for eating? Why bother fishing at all? This sounds a whole lot easier, than regular fishing. A guy could just take a half-ton truck, back it in close, and start chucking in fish." (the renowned pitchfork method)

Thudder regurgitated his mother's explanation, "I don't know for sure, but Mom said the fish are no good for eating when they're spawning, like they're all soft, or poisonous, or something. I'm not sure if it's true or not."

"I think the whole thing is baloney, actually, Thudder. I think you're the one that would believe anything." Mac was always having fun with truth, and exaggeration, in its many forms. Exaggeration, after all, is only a big version of truth. (Logically then, is truth just mini-exaggeration?)

"Well, another time, a relative of mine told me about a river in Lumsden, Saskatchewan, flooding its banks in the springtime, and there were fish going through the streets, so much that the kids got pitchforks, and were spear-fishing with the pitchforks. I've also heard that same story about stream outlets at lakes, like Pigeon Lake."

Mac laughed. "Ha. Ha. So you are gullible?"

Thudder spoke a bit defensively. "Well, you never know about these things.

Stranger things have happened. I've seen the salmon spawning stuff on the films at school. They do congregate in swirling masses."

Mac chuckled again. "Ha. Ha. You just admitted that you actually watch those films in school. Good boy. I am proud of you."

Thudder defended himself some more. "Oh, but that was back when I was about grade four. Of course I don't watch those films now. You probably watched those films in grade four, too. As I recall, you were just a goody-goody little kid always sucking up to the teacher."

"Yep. Just like you."

Thudder, who had been watching for the road that he thought was the right road, announced, "Hey, I think this is it. Turn south here."

Mac did as he was told, and pulled his old Valiant off the highway. After a few miles, they came to a short rustic bridge, and an old sign that indicated it was the Ribstone Creek. He stopped the car, and they got out to investigate. Thudder looked from the top of the bridge into the murky water below. "Well, I sure don't see anything here."

"Surprise, surprise." Mac indicated the correctness of his prediction, that they were on a stupid myth-discovering wild goose chase.

"Well, as I remember, there were plains, sort of, and lots of grass, you know, like muskeg, sort of, where the water spreads out. But I don't see anything like that around here. Let's drive over another mile or so to the next road."

Mac questioned this decision somewhat. "Like I said before, we can drive around out here all day. There is a north-south road every mile. We could go back and forth all the way to the Saskatchewan border. How many of these roads do you want to check out?"

Thudder was a bit discouraged. It seemed this childhood question that had been plaguing him all these years was going to be one that he might have to take to the grave. "Just one more, then. And if that place isn't it, I'll hint around to Mom. But her memory for roads is even worse than mine. She can get lost in *town*, for crying out loud. Maybe we could ask some old farmers. They'd know for sure."

"There is no way I'm going into a farmer's yard and asking, 'Have you seen a bunch of jackfish spawning anywhere around here?' The guy would think we had been taking drugs." Mac chuckled at the thought of the farmer's dumb flabbergasted look.

"Well," Thudder went on. "So what? The farmer doesn't know you or me from a hole in the ground, and if he thinks we're nuts, that's his problem. On the other hand, if the fish story is true, he might be able to point us right to the right place. I'll ask him. You can stay in the car, if you like."

Sure enough, as they headed back north one road over from the previous one, there was an old somewhat dilapidated farmhouse nestled on the south slope of the gentle dip that held the Ribstone. "Drive in there." Thudder pointed to the farmhouse. "Like I said, you can stay in the car."

"Well, I admire your determination. Go for it. I'll turn the car around cause if they think you're nuts, or dangerous, or drunk, you can run, and we'll beat it out of here." Clearly, Mac was enjoying his pal's will to find out the truth about this legend.

Thudder approached the farmhouse, and was greeted by a mongrel, that was 50% growler, and 50% tailwagger. Never sure regarding canine greetings, Thudder beckoned. "Hi, Boy," in his best dogfriendly tone. The mutt slowly transformed into 100% tailwagger, and Thudder breathed a sigh of relief, as he began stroking the animal's head.

An older woman opened the door cautiously. "Can I help you, Young Man?"

Thudder didn't really know how to start this perhaps ridiculous request. "Well, a long time ago my mother lived along here somewhere, and she said that fish congregate to spawn somewhere along here. My friend and are just out for a drive to see if we can check it out. Have you ever heard any stories like that?"

The old woman smiled. Obviously a pleasant memory had surfaced. "Well, yes. It happened in the old days. It's been a long time since we were out there. It's a ways from here. Back then, some years, all kinds of people would go, just to watch, you know. If you come inside for a minute, I can draw you a map of how to get there. You did get the right time of year. Right about now."

Thudder felt relieved. Someone else actually backed the story. He stepped inside.

Meanwhile, back in the car, Mac had been approached by the mutt-mongrel. For some reason, the canine had taken a nasty stance towards Mac, much differently than for Thudder. Perhaps it was Mac's higher voice, or showing of distrust. Regardless, Mac was not about to step out of the car, with this vicious snarling animal glaring its sharp looking teeth at him. Farm dogs, so territorial, are a weird unpredictable lot, and he knew it. He preferred to keep his skin intact, free from bite marks.

Thudder returned to pat the mutt, much to Mac's dismay. He carried a piece of old paper in his hand. When he got back into the car, his excitement was evident. "She said it's true. At least in the old days. She doesn't know if it still happens or not, but she drew me a map, and told me how to get to the spot."

"Well okay, then. Either she knew it was a bullshit story, and strung you along, or it's true. Only one thing to do, then. Navigate me there. You are going to get your answer, one way or another, I guess."

"Go back south to the next road over." Thudder gave the first direction.

The mates drove a few more miles, and arrived back at the creek's gully. To the east were flats that appeared to be a likely spot, and matched the description that the farm lady had given Thudder. Thudder pointed in that general direction. There was a three-foot bank from which they could have a gander. Mac pulled the car onto an approach. "Let's walk from here."

It took about five minutes for the pair to arrive at the scene. Sure enough, down in the shallow creek, were fish, literally hundreds of fish. Big pike. Little pike. Mid-sized pike. Dumb pike all. 'Stupitus uglicus' at it's remarkable natural reproductive process. The amazed wild goose hunting duo just stood and watched, not knowing what to think or say, like the first time an urchin sees the mountains, or a picture of a naked lady.

As they had not carried any gum boots, the sole way to check this out more closely would be to rollup the pant-legs, or just take the pants off, and wade in, in shorts. Being modest fellows, they just kicked off shoes and socks, and rolled up their pant-legs. Curiousity as to the lethargy of the fish overwhelmed them, and they plunged in together. Sure enough Mother had been accurate. Thudder proved it by reaching down with both hands as a football centre would hike the ball, grabbed a massive slippery pike, and heaved it up onto the grass, just to prove that this was possible. The pike flopped around some, and finally made its flopping way back to the edge of the short bank, and flipped in.

"Fish fight!" yelled Thudder, as he tossed a scrawnier one off in Mac's direction. It struck Mac across his butt, as he had bent to retrieve another monster. Chaos ruled for the next few minutes, as the two lads launched the fish around, hither and thither, and pretended the fish were swords, to fight with. They contested who could grab the longest one, and took turns smearing each other with the stinky slime from the muck. Glorious, glorious, natural guck. Pigs in muck. Kids in dirtpiles. Scrooge in money. Mac and Thudder in a whopping pile of fish!

The slimy, gooey, and sticky creatures had no way of running from the shallows, and these fiendish humans they had unfortunately encountered. Their recourse was only that soon the two fellows had slipped into the mucky murky mess, and had encountered the slime, the eggs, and the stench. Fish revenge. "We'll make that sucker's car stink. We'll make their clothes reek. They'll regret this."

Smeared with guck up to their necks, the pair proved once again that humans, (as if we need proof) when given the correct conditions, will wallow in slime as well as any other species, even swine. Just as we say 'swine are clean animals when given the chance', swine can say 'men are pigs if given the chance'.

The fishfrolicking duo eventually tired of the frivolity, and retired to the nearby bank to just enjoy watching this amazing act of nature. "Well, now do you believe me?" asked Thudder.

"Yep. I do." Mac looked at him. "Seems to me we are going to have a hard time convincing too many others, though. Unless you want me to bring others out here, and from the smell of both of us, I'm not so sure about that."

"You've convinced girls to go out with you," said Thudder. "Anything's possible."

"Yeah, I guess," agreed Mac. "But this one's gonna need a real straight face."

End of an Era - The Last Net

The standard nutrient rich Youngman breakfast fare consisted of hotcakes, maple syrup, strong coffee, and stronger moonshine.

Willy and Richard were pumped, if you could call it that. Two days earlier, the trusty net had yielded 34 fish, enough to have a veritable fresh feast, and still have a few left for the freezer. That freezer sure was a darn lot simpler than smoking them, or worse, pickling them. That net too was immensely more prolific than the hook and line method. Too bad it only worked real decent in the spring. Even then, though, it hadn't always worked, thanks to human interference from somewhere, up on the other side. Once some diphead thieving farmer guys had raided the thing. But that was just once, a few years back. The brothers Youngman had become paranoid then of being reported to the wildlife officers, and had been more cautious since. But as time passed, their caution dissipated, and their wanton use of the net continued without fear, as if it were up north, on the settlement, and legal. Besides, if the fish didn't hit it in the spring run towards cleaner water up the creek, they could always use it midsummer across the river itself. This was never as successful, but still the odd dufus fish would enter the pits of net.

Still Willy reminisced about the old days, back when they were kids, up north, and when they had first moved here, too. "You know, Richard, I miss those smoked fish some days. They were tastier that way. You used willow, or birch. Remember?"

"But you never did any of the work, Willy. I always did all of the skinning, hanging, and smoking. I like the freezer method." Richard was the lazy but dumber guy, often manipulated into doing far more than his share of any of the work.

"I don't know if it's all that easier, Richard. We still have to catch the fish, and filet them. Maybe just once, you could smoke a few more just for me? Wouldn't you like to do a kind thing for your brother?"

"If you want to eat smoked fish, why don't you smoke them yourself, eh?" Richard, as usual, was determined not to be had, at least this early, before he yet had half a stupor up, from the moonshine. By the time the stupor came on, which was usually about noon, he might be more amiable to the brother's requests. In fact, unless today was vastly different than any other, it would be true. Noon equals stupor time.

"Maybe we could have a little bet, then, something that has to do with the

106

fish, at the creek, this morning." Lately Willy had taken to letting Richard even suggest the nature of the bets, and then distorting it so he could win. Each day, or twice a day, because their life was just so darn boring, they had some kind of goofy bet. In the beginning Willy almost always won. But that was changing. Either Richard was slowly becoming wiser with each new way of losing, or Willy was gaining some compassion for the poor sot of a brother, and allowing him to win a bit more.

Richard maintained his unwillingness to participate this morning, as usual. "I don't feel like betting. Besides, another way you can get smoked fish is to buy some at the store. It's pretty good, eh?"

There was hope for Willy yet. If Richard had another weakness, besides being a dullard head, it was that he did have some pride in his earthy abilities, at least some of them. He was darn good at tasting moonshine, for example. Willy complimented him, "Ah, Richy, that bought stuff is so salty. It comes from the ocean, you know. It is nowhere near as good as your smoked fish. Yours is special. It's the best in all of Western Canada, I bet. If some guys ever had a smoked fish contest, you would surely win."

At this, Richard's ears perked up, for the first time today. "Really, Willy? You really think so?"

Willy glared, defiant at the suggestion he might distort truth. "Jeez, Richard, you know better than that. Old Willy here would never lie to you about something like that." Of course, if it involved some work being transferred off of Willy on to Richard, the BS lies could evolve to the expensive Charolais-like type, not just your ordinary BS, but quality BS. Willy, after all, *had* to do some of the work, for he was the only one with any degree of literacy. To Willy, he was the brains, and Richard was the brawn.

"That looks like rhubarb, Dad." Walter Brock was staring out the window of his car, as the pair approached the old bridge above the creek.

"I believe it is, Son."

"So there must have been a homestead here once, then?" Walter, back from the city, always enjoyed discussing the history of the place. It was a fascinating topic, and provided conversation. At least it was a whole lot better than if they talked about Johnny's life, which was a failure, and had been one ever since he'd left the farm. (Any move away from the farm was a failure, in some eyes.) Dad was familiar with all kinds of beat-up roads, and trails, that curved past old concrete and brick foundations, and rusted threshing machines. He knew which farmers' "No Trespassing!" signs were serious and which weren't. Each old foundation or caragana bush was a trace of mans' settlement of the valley, and each had its unique story, some sad, some true, and now, from Dad, many a whole lot of altered bull.

If Dad didn't have the truth, he could at least invent a close-truth. "Well, according to my dad, your grandfather, there used to be an old guy named Perkins that lived there. Supposedly he was a moonshiner, and he used rhubarb

107

somehow in the process. Dad never spoke of it much. My guess is he wouldn't have liked it, but didn't know what to do. Times then were different."

"You mean your Dad would have been against the making of it, or he just wouldn't have liked the taste?"

"As far as I know, no one liked the taste. They drank it for the wallop. Same as booze today. For the most part, my grandfather, your great grandfather, so I hear, was really strict. I heard once that he tried to let the officials know about the moonshine. I don't know much, really. I doubt that Dad would have done anything like that."

"And you?" Walter asked.

"Well, it was before my time, but I probably would have gone on down, and found it, and tried to steal some."

Walter reflected, and the topic changed, as the truck approached the bridge. "Those were more interesting times, I think. Were there fish in the river then, too?"

"Oh, I imagine so, but we never went fishing. I guess not too many people knew. Somebody must have discovered it some time along the way, I suppose. I imagine it goes in cycles. The river can get really low some years."

"So do you think there will be any fish there this year?"

"You never know, eh? We'll just have to check it out, won't we? It doesn't matter. I'm enjoying the drive. This is the trail to the mouth." He pointed to the right, "If there are any fish, I'll catch them before you."

Walter slowed down, and exited the gravel road to the dirt two-track trail.

Eglinton Brock spoke. "It's about a mile down to the mouth, if I remember right."

"I'm sure you will remember, Dad. You always remember." Walter reassured his father, who really didn't need reassuring. Still, silence was broken with the unimportant trivial conversations of giving directions, and reminiscing. A lot better than discussing politics or religion. The generation gap had gotten larger with each generation.

But recreational activities such as fishing were escapes from any conflict, and were far more bonding. Soon the father-son duo arrived at the creek's mouth. Walter stared straight at the water. "Look at that. Somebody has a net in here."

"Well, I'll be. I thought that those things had gone away a long time ago. About the same time as moonshine disappeared." Eglinton was legitimately surprised.

"So Richard, can you think of something we can bet about?" Willy had yet to organise the brother into the work, or any smoking of fish.

"I told you I don't want to bet today, Willy. The only bet is I bet I will lose the bet."

"Well, then you would win for sure, Richard. Cause if you bet you'd lose, and then you did lose, you would win the bet that you would lose. Therefore, you'd win. That sounds like a way you couldn't lose, eh? That's pretty darn smart of you, I think." Willy used flattery, besides word confusion, whenever possible, as one of the duping tricks up his sleeve.

Richard looked up from his moonshine mug, and his jaw dropped, while his eyes widened. One eyebrow twisted upwards in that sure sign to Willy that stupor time was close at hand, if not already here. "Uhhh," he moaned, "I think I just want to go check on the net. Is it time?"

"So you aren't going to smoke any fish for us?"

"Nope." Richard spoke in direct monosyllables when his mind was made up.

"I figured that. Tell you what, Little Brother. How's this? I'll BET you that you won't smoke any fish." Willy stressed the word 'BET'. If there was one thing Richard hated even more than working for Willy, it was losing bets to Willy.

"I don't like it when you call me Little Brother. I'm bigger and tougher than you. I just want to go check on our net. There must be fish in it by now. And I don't want to bet."

"Even if you're guaranteed to win the bet?"

"Well, that might be different." Intelligence wise, Richard was somewhat like the fish, being drawn towards the net. In fact, between the walleye, and the pike, Richard was somewhere in between. Perhaps he was just a white sucker, not as voracious as the pike, but not as wily as the walleye, either.

Willy stood from his end of the table, confident that by the time they got home, he would have the poor fellow convinced of the worthiness of any fish smoking labour the sot could be brought to do. "Let's go, then. I've been ready all along. Grab that jar of shine. We're going to get a lot of those big fat jack today. The better kind for smoking. Maybe we could hang them up somehow above the still, and let the soak up some of that smoke. Do you think it would work?"

Richard yawned. "Nope. You need more smoke than that. You don't know nothing about smoking fish, do you?"

"That's cause when we were kids, you were Mom's little boy, and always hung out with her, and I went out with Dad, fishing, and hunting."

Richard hated teasing mostly because he didn't understand it. "One of these days, Willy, if you weren't my brother, I'd just up and clobber you. Sometimes you really p___ me off."

And so the tradition continued. The spring rites of netting fish, and the Youngman brothers debating a bet. If the boys could have kept track, this was their 23rd year of harvesting the gilled bounty from the creek. Richard and Willy could have been professionals at that. Fortunately, somehow they always seemed to limit their arguing and fighting just enough that their mere survival wasn't threatened. It was close, sometimes, but yes, the desire to live was still ahead. It was almost brotherly love.

Eglinton Brock recognised what to do. Perhaps the strictness of his ancestors had left his mind, but there was still honour and law, even in the more sporty endeavours, like fishing. "Son, I hate to tell you this, but the sight of that thing really eats me. I thought those things were long gone. It's still legal up north on reserves, and in lakes, if you have a commercial license. But here for sure it's illegal, not to mention unethical. Guys like this spoil nature for the rest of us. Half the lakes and streams will be pure catch and release in a few years.

"So what do we do about it then?" Walter sought more information on the plan.

"Look around. Do you see any other people? Not me. We're going to stop these fellows once and for all, whoever they are. Get your sharpest knife out of your tackle box. Better yet, why don't you look in my toolbox for the tin-snips, or a pair of scissors? Something that will cut. I'll pull the net."

"I get it, Dad," said Walter. "I just hope we don't get caught. But I think maybe we should just take it with us."

"But I want to leave these guys a real hard message, and that is that we totally disapprove. Besides, if we took it with us, we might get caught with it. Possession is most of ownership."

Walter did as he was told, even though he was an adult now, capable of his own moral decisions. Still, he took orders from Dad, as he always had. One day he might, with some romance luck, get one of his own kids to boss around. Then it would all balance out.

Eglinton poked himself over to the net, and found the correct line to untie to pull the contraption in. "There are some nice fish in it, Son. When you get over here, I want you to go down by the water, and as I pull them in, you can release them all. I think that it's only fair if they were caught illegally, they get to go."

"Yeah, it seems too bad we can't keep them, but then we'd be illegal too, I guess."

When the fish were released, the Brocks took to the net, like little kids wrecking of the girl's fort, or just plain wrecking. It's innate in boys and men, this uncontrollable wanting reckless abandon to wreck something, be it that first tower of blocks, or an old car being shoved off a cliff. Except this time the Brocks didn't have to feel guilty. There was just cause for the destruction. The pair hacked, cut, and chopped the poor netting entirely into small bits, leaving nothing but a pile of knots, each with four tassels hanging out. They piled the stringy mess on the summit of the gentle hillock near the creek, on the most prominent portion of land, hoping to shock the net owner guys, totally.

Eglinton looked at the pile they had made, partly with accomplishment, but still mostly in disdain. He had that 'That'll show those bastards!' look on his face. "Now I don't even feel like fishing here. Besides, those idiots might come look for their net. What do you say we drive upstream and try the other creek mouth? Start fresh, like."

"Sounds good to me, Dad." Walter had already accomplished the main goal of getting in a visit. The rest was bonus.

Willy Youngman started the truck, and Richard jumped in the passenger side, as always. Occasionally he would ask Willy if he could drive, but a quick cuff on the side of the head normally stopped that idea. Technically, and legally, they were partners. They held joint ownership to everything that was theirs. Richard had somehow managed that much.

They hadn't been going to town much lately, nor up north to see relatives. The bar guy had put them on his black list for too much fighting, so they had to always go to the government vendors for any booze, just in case they wanted a break from the hard stuff, their moonshine. Life had been pretty ordinary, and easy. They had leased out their land to a neighbour farmer who then did all the work, and paid them a share. TV had been a real godsend for their natural sloth-fulness.

As soon as the truck got some of that blue smoke spouting out the back, Willy's tongue started to roll, "So Richard. Here's the deal. "I will BET you that you definitely won't smoke any fish. In fact I BET that you can't even remember how, you're getting so old and lazy."

"You think I can't remember how to smoke fish?" He disapproved of memory insults, although from all that moonshine, certainly he had lost a memory or two along with the brain cells.

"Yep. We've had that freezer at least ten years. So it's been more than ten years since you smoked any."

Richard was quicker than normal this morning. "Well, I know I can, and I don't need to bet for that."

"Tell you what. If you promise to smoke even one fish for me, I'll let you drive the truck home." Willy dealt two high cards at once: the truck, and the supposedly no-lose bet. Richard cherished driving the truck, and if he smoked one fish, it would be a simple matter to convince him to smoke the rest.

"Just one fish?"

"Yep. Just one fish." reiterated Willy.

"And what do I get, again?"

"You get to drive the truck. I told you that before." Willy made it sound like a great deal.

"Okay, then I'll do it. But that's all. Can we shake on it?"

Willy reached over, and gave the usual strong firm, but still meaningless, as always, handshake to his brother.

Richard laughed. "Ha. I fooled ya."

"How come?" inquired Willy.

Richard took pride in his outsmarting his brother this time, if only within his own child logic. "We never agreed on who was going to eat the smoked fish, and it's gonna be me."

"How do you know I won't eat it before you?"

"Cause you're so stupid that you'll eat it raw, before it's done, cause you don't know how to tell when it's done, and I do."

"I might just call the deal off, then." Willy often called deals off, and always did when they weren't at all in his favour. He evoked the constitutional power of the King Youngman, or at least the Smarter Youngman.

"But we shook on it, Willy. Too bad."

The pair had by now arrived at their secret and sacred netting grounds, and crawled out of the half-ton. Richard was the first to see it. "What's that pile of rubbish there, Willy?"

Willy squinted, and looked closer. "It looks like an old net, or something."

Then Richard stared over at the poles where their net had been hanging for the past week or so. "Damn, Willy. Our net is missing too."

In the meantime, Willy was having a closer inspection at the cut up pile of mesh. "This is OUR net, Richard. Some bastards cut the heck out of our net!"

Richard kicked the ground. "Son of a bitch. I wish I could get my hands on them right now. I'd let them know what I think of this."

"And if you didn't, I sure the hell would, Richard. Go get the rest of that shine. I NEED some! Bad!"

Richard did as he was told. He split the remainder of the ketchup bottle of white sparkly liquid into the two coffee mugs. He handed one to Richard, who was sitting on the now dry pile of net, looking reminiscent, and reflecting on how they could recreate the bounty.

"That's the only net. We'd have to go up north and get us another one," he said.

"It was a damn good net, too, Willy. It caught us a lot of fish over the years. In fact, I remember only once when those other guys took fish from it. We probably have caught at least a thousand fish with it, eh?"

"Yeah, something like that, Richard. And I was looking forward to your good smoked fish today. Damn, I'll miss that, Richard."

"You mean you'll miss watching me do all the work, like usual."

"No, Richy, not at all. This stuff is fun, and that's the part I'll miss." Willy could get serious.

But Richard was smiling over something. "Well, at least I sort of won the bet. I won't be smoking no fish today, eh?"

"Yes, Richard. You kind of won the bet again, you dumb little brother. I bet you you wouldn't be smoking any fish so I won, too. It's sort of a tie." Willy went over, wanting to give the sad ol' guy a brotherly hug, but backed off when Richard backed away. To be sad was one thing. To hug over it was another completely. These girl emotions would have to stay bottled up a while longer. After all, they were men.

Willy sprinkled the remainder of his moonshine onto the pile of mesh, and reached for the matches in his shirt pocket. Then he bent down and ignited the moonshine, and it quickly spread to the dry string, and burlap, encompassing the whole of netting history, here at the Mouth, with it, as it burned.

Then he turned sadly to little Richard, who had a tear in his eye. "You can drive home anyway, Richard. I'll let you."

"And I would have cooked you the best smoked fish ever, Willy. You better believe it."

The Crush Goddess

Ever since the time they had ridden along the river, Becky and Anne had made it their favoured exploration spot. That day they had discovered so much, about herons, about bats, and even some about adult behaviour, although part of them wished they hadn't. Certainly they were beholden to Mom for allowing the river as a new exploration destination.

Vacation school started smooth, although they found it extremely difficult to even talk to Miss Davis, so that relationship, having started out in such an unusual way, floundered. (The girls had unintentionally observed Miss Davis skinny-dipping) On the way to the first class, Anne had said, "I'm not going to talk to Miss Davis at all. I'm scared that I'll start giggling or look embarrassed, and she'll pry, and the whole scary story will come tumbling out."

Becky had agreed. "Me, too. That's for sure. We'll have to make sure to spend all of our time with the other kids."

Gladys was disappointed that the two Sampson girls were so aloof, but she had thought to herself before, that not everyone would be overtly friendly, or necessarily easy to deal with. After Day One, she concluded, while reflecting on it in the evening, that the boys in her class were more amiable. In fact they were, although she wasn't completely aware of the reasons. This teaching role was unfamiliar to her, and she had not had any experience dealing with young boys in teacher/student mode. Due to their overwhelming almost sickening crushes on the attractive preacher, once that initial embarrassment and shyness was overcome, the boys became the ones who went pretend-begging to her for help. They shyly approached for assistance, in the hopes of getting a whiff of her exquisite perfume, or better yet, a touch, or glancing body rub, or a touch of her skirt. She was the Crush Goddess, and she didn't realise it. Lyle seemed to be smitten the worst. He was younger than some of the others, and therefore less reserved about it.

Becky and Anne had to take back stage, at least until they were accustomed to observing Miss Davis with her clothes on instead of off. After about a week, the memories of seeing her naked wore off, and were replaced with more mental, emotional qualities. Things warmed up between the three of them.

On the first weekend, Becky and Anne talked about how the first week had gone. "Anne," Becky said, "remember when we were down by the river that day, before we ran into them? Remember when we had the idea about putting messages into bottles? I think we should suggest that to Miss Davis on Monday. Maybe the last day, on Friday, the whole class could go down to the river, and throw in bottles. Let's ask Mom first, cause we'll probably have to ask her to drive."

The girls approached their Mother, "Mom, we had this idea, the other day when we were riding our bikes along the river, that for vacation school, we could all write notes in bottles and send them down the river. What do you think?"

Mrs. Sampson really liked her kids' ideas, but she also had another role to play, being one of the church's elders, and in this case she had to fill in a report on Miss Davis. "I think that's a great idea, Girls. Why don't you present it to your teacher tomorrow? She'll have to be the one that decides for sure, because she's the teacher."

Anne continued, "Will you help drive then, if it's okay with her? That will make the organising part easier."

"Sure." Mom smiled at their sweetness, still oblivious to their lost innocence, of the previous week. Anne and Becky too were pleased to distance themselves from the memories of Miss Davis splashing around in the buff at the river.

The next day the girls' brilliant plan was presented and accepted. The boys thought it was pretty stupid, but that was mostly because Miss Davis's attention was shifting away from them, and onto the girls. It was just horrible, for Lyle. She was the only reason he came at all. All the Bible stuff, and arts and crafts were a major inconvenience to being around her and staring at her comely face. Everyone except Miss Davis knew that he was enamoured. Homework was assigned that each child was to bring back a bottle, one that had a really decent top that screwed on, or a good cork that wouldn't come out easily. Becky suggested moreover that it would be better if they were the clear glass kind, not the brown ones, and then the students could put in coloured notes, which strangers in some dreamy far off place downstream would be more likely to discover.

On Tuesday, after noticing some of the labels, Miss Davis quietly announced. "The first thing we all need to do is to scrub all these bottles really clean, and that includes taking off the paper labels, too." Somehow, it didn't seem appropriate that a church summer school should be sending out notes in bottles of Five Star Whiskey or Lamb's Navy Rum. These liquor bottles were, however, excellent bottles, well suited to the purpose, especially the 12 ouncers, as they were flat, and would float along well. If the labels remained, the people who spot them might think that that's quite the church going on upstream. Perhaps they have their sermons Saturday nights instead of Sunday mornings.

On Tuesday evening Miss Davis phoned Tom Jackson, her new found friend-perhaps-more, hoping he would be able to volunteer on Friday at noon as an extra driver. "Tom, on Friday, the children are all going down to the river. They've all prepared bottles with notes in them, and we're going to celebrate the end of vacation school with a picnic, and casting in the bottles. They're all excited. Do you think you could come along?"

"Actually, Gladys, I have something else to do that day. I have to pick up my cousin in Edmonton. He's come from Seattle on the train through Vancouver. He's coming to stay for a few days. I'll have to get him settled in. I'd really like to, but I have to say I can't. I'll probably be able to make it to church on Sunday, though."

Gladys was a bit disappointed, as she thought she did want to see the refreshing fellow again. After all, she had taken pleasure from their other outing immensely, having found another side to life, with him. It had been stressful in the beginning though, making the choice, and having everything happen so darn fast. "It's okay. I'm sure I can find someone else to drive the kids. Lots of Moms will be available, I'm sure."

Tom wasn't all that sorry. He was kind of sick of kids for now, having taught them all year, and surely Roland, the cousin, would be bringing along some weed. (marijuana) It had been awhile since he'd smoked up. Perhaps they would get a hotel in Edmonton, and have a rousing night on the town. Perhaps even, they might luck onto a couple of willing girls in some bar. He was hoping so anyway. If not the girls, at least he'd have some weed to enjoy, and some stories to share with Roland.

116

Wednesday was the day that the creative notes were made up, and placed inside the bottles of mystery. Miss Davis gave the instructions. "I'm not going to read your notes unless you want me to, or you need help. Remember to put today's date down which is July 22, 1966. You should address it to, "Whomever finds this bottle," and you should request that they write you back at your address. You should also write something about yourself."

Lyle wrote: (spelling is as he wrote it)
"July 22, 1966. My nam is Lyle. I am puting a note in a botle because the most beutiful girl in the world, Miss Davis, askt me to. One day when I grow up I will mary her. Write to me, plese. Signed, Lyle Johnstone."
Then he left his address.

Anne wrote:
"To the finder of this bottle:
I hope you are a wonderful curious handsome person. I have dropped this bottle into the Battle River near Forestburg, Alberta. Please write to me if you find this bottle and note. I hope it gets all the way to Hudson's Bay. We are doing this for a Vacation School Project on July 22, 1966. If you write to me nicely, I'll tell you a crazy secret about my Vacation Bible school teacher, Miss Davis, and my regular teacher, Mr. Jackson.

Yours Truly, Miss Anne Sampson."

Little Ralph got assistance from Miss Davis. He proudly sat on her lap while she held his hand to write the words clearly.
"To whomever finds this note: Today is July 22, 1966. Please write to me, Ralph Cameron, RR1, Forestburg, Alberta. I am having fun at Vacation Bible School. Good-bye." Then he drew a crooked picture of Miss Davis, and the church. Miss Davis stood as tall as the church, and had a whole lot more brilliance to her. Her lines were more exquisite. Ralph took about a hundred times more time drawing her than he had for the poor church. He might as well have drawn the outhouse, for how it appeared.

On Friday, all the students brought wonderful old time lunches to share, in their school lunch-kits. Before this day, Vacation School had ended at 11:30 each forenoon and they had all gone home for lunch. Moms always competed at these times, to see whose sandwiches, and baked snacks could be the most marvelled at, and talked about. So the assemblage was sure to be dining on exquisite fare. About eleven o'clock, the entire cast of characters piled into the three cars to head down to the river, for the picnic lunches, and the ritualistic casting off of the magical bottles, as if it were truly from a story book, not reality. Miss Davis had gone over to the rural store the evening before to get them all Crush sodas for her treat, it being the last day of vacation school,

117

and all. She had been to enough of these events as a student, that she was familiar with such cordiality.

Becky and Anne asked their Mom if they could journey to the river in Miss Davis's car. Mom expressed that that would be fine, so the two girls crawled into the back seat, and lucky little Lyle got to sit in the front beside the Goddess, who today was decked out in the most glorious flowing flowery dress he'd ever seen. He couldn't talk, so she did.

"Does your family ever go down to this river, Lyle? I understand there are some delightful spots along it, for picnicking."

Lyle wanted to say so much, but all he could muster beyond his ogle, and choking throat was a quiet "Yes, Ma'am." The poor guy was flustered from his toes to his ears. If he'd been 14, the sweat from his armpits would have been staining her car.

So she turned her attention to the back seat. "What about you girls? Do you go down to the river much?"

Anne glanced at Becky, in the knowledge that this conversation had a possible deadly end. "Well, yes. Mom let us go this year by ourselves on our bikes for the first time."

"Oh, really. When did you first get to go?"

Anne paused, then lied. "A couple of weeks ago we rode along the road between the two bridges."

Anne's words made Gladys suddenly realise that her little venture with Mr. Jackson wasn't quite so safe as she had previously thought. Her childhood memories of the quietness of bicycling came rushing back, too vividly. She imagined they very well could have snuck up on she and Tom, the wild teacher guy. She abruptly changed the conversation. "So are you looking forward to putting in the bottles? It was such a neat idea the two of you had!"

Becky's face showed some relief at the sway in the discussion. "Yes, we are. It's fun imagining how far they could go. The other day we had a map of Western Canada, and were looking at all the places the bottles could end up."

Miss Davis admired the intelligence of the pair, and hadn't realised just how smart kids can be, until this week. What they came up with amazed her. "You could have brought the map to Vacation School."

"Oh no," Anne giggled. "That would have made it far too much like real school. Vacation School is supposed to be fun."

Agreeing with Anne's insight, Miss Davis, too, giggled. At this, Lyle looked up at the giggling Goddess, wishing he could be about fifteen years older, right now. Her giggling made her more attractive than ever. This was the last day, too. He knew he had to do something more, if he was to get her to notice him, as a man.

The poor student minister didn't realise just quite how excited this bottle-tossing event would be, and wasn't exactly prepared for the commotion that ensued upon their arrival. She stepped out of the car, to an awaiting whirling throb of screaming questioning excitement.

"Can we throw them now?"

"Can we go back up on the bridge?"

"What if they don't float?"

"What part of the river?"

"Stop pushing, would you, Lyle?"

"Can we swim after?"

"But I can't swim."

"Mine's the bestest!"

"Is not!"

"Mine will float the farthest!"

"Yours will sink."

"I hope yours sinks."

She wished they would all just shut the heck up, and sit down on the grass, like obedient Children of God. This display wouldn't go over well with Mrs. Sampson, who was the church elder who would be filing her report. So she did the wise mature thing. She waited. The two mom's stared down their own kids, and those in turn put fingers to mouths to inform everyone else to shut up. Eventually the calamity subsided enough so she could address them.

"I stopped here last night, in fact, and I thought quite a bit about it. It wouldn't be smart to toss them off the bridge because they might very well break. We don't want anyone being disappointed at that. Actually what we should do is place them in the part of the river where there is more current. That way they will get a good start. So I want all of you to look out at the river, and decide which part has the best current. When you've decided, raise your hand, and we'll discuss whether or not you're right."

Lyle shot up his had right away, and blurted, "Right in the very middle!"

"I'm sorry, Lyle. You're going to have to look a bit closer than that."

Lyle's face went sour. He had wanted to impress her, any way he could, and he thought he should have been able, this river stuff being more of a boy thing and all.

Anne raised her hand, and spoke, articulately, "If you watch the flow of the water closely, you can see that it's over near the other side, about ten feet out into the water."

The Goddess smiled. (Although she had lost much of her Goddess status in Lyle's eyes, temporarily, at least. But Crush Goddesses tend to have their faults dissipate quickly.) "Yes, that's what I thought last night. So what we have to do is go over the bridge, which will be a nice walk anyway, and then we can simply toss them all gently out from that shore."

The stroll over was a race, for the boys. They jostled for position to impress the Goddess, who didn't notice them at all. Lyle was bounced by a bigger chap, and tripped. He grimaced bravely as he rose to continue. The girls, more cultured, walked beside Miss Davis, and the two Moms. Boys in jeans tumbled off the end of the bridge, and down through some tall grass to the Battle's edge. They managed somehow to avoid pushing one another in.

When Miss Davis arrived, she called, "One at a time, now. You don't want the bottles smashing each other. Little ones first. Say a silent prayer to yourself for the bottle, as you toss them."

As each child tossed his or her art project out into the river, a mild round of applause droned through the wind. No doubt those bottles would be successful in their maiden voyages downstream along the mighty Battle, dweeb river that it was. They were sure to wander far, to mystical magical kingdoms, like Hardisty, Fabyan, or North Battleford. (Or at least until somewhere around the next bend.)

The fifteen handsome decked-out people headed back across the bridge, this time the older boys lingering below, hoping in fact for a brilliant gust of wind to come along and make those pretty dresses perform a bit.

Alas, it didn't happen, to the chagrin of the peeping toms below. They needed some lessons from Anne and Becky.

The mothers helped Miss Davis spread out the blankets for the picnic, and set out the lunches. Each child found a spot, and the entire cast rejoiced in the grace of God. Except for Lyle. He sat over on the grass, on a hillock by himself, just looking out at the river. Miss Davis noticed, and called, "Sure you don't want to join us, Lyle?"

There was no reply. He just kept staring off. This moping sulking boy was unfamiliar to her. There was no apparent reason for this. The bottles, the outing, the car ride. All of it added up to joyousness. Sure, they all might be a bit sad that this was the last day, but surely it wasn't all that bad. After staring inquisitively at him for a moment longer, she glanced over at Anne's mom, Mrs. Sampson, who in turn motioned her head sideways to indicate they should go for a short private walk.

Gladys left her blanket spot, and joined Anne's mother. Out of hearing range of the others, the older child-wise experienced woman spoke, "I think he has a crush on you, and he's hurting, probably because you're leaving, and maybe some things have gone bad for him today."

The minister had a puzzled look. She hadn't been around adoring little boys much. In fact, never. She looked at Mrs. Sampson for the answer. "So what is one to do about this?"

"There's not a whole lot you can do. He'll get over it, for sure. You can try explaining it to him, but that probably won't work. Often that'll make him think you care for him even more. The thing you need to realise most that any injury to his feelings isn't your fault at all, and he'll get over it, probably sooner than you think."

"Okay, then. Thanks, Mom, for your advice."

Mrs. Sampson smiled in appreciation of the honorary 'Mom' title.

Back at the picnic spot, the picnickers were finishing up, and began packing, enjoying the Orange Crush soda treats that Miss Davis handed out. But not Lyle.

Of course, the irate one, in his scowling, received his cool treat last, because he lined up last, and then blamed this on her, mistakenly deducing that she liked him the very least of all the children. Pouts and crushes evoke such ridiculous fancy. The pout continued to the bitter end. He gave Ralph a shove, closed his fist when Becky tried to ask him what was wrong, and had his lower lip far enough out for a bird to land on, and pick his nose for him. Clearly, this was not his day. He was somehow coaxed back into the Goddess-become-She-Devil's car for the long trip back to the church, mostly because the other cars were full, and he thought she hated him so much she might just leave him behind to limp all the way home by his wretched self.

The three cars arrived in a small procession back at church, where parents were waiting to give thanks to the young minister for her patience and skill at schooling the youth for the two weeks. Coincidentally, Lyle's mother was late, and Miss Davis found herself alone with the wee pouter of a lad, in an uncomfortable space, on one hand wishing to make him feel better, yet not wanting to make it worse either. She had no clue what to do.

But Lyle made the first move. "Did you like my bottle?" he asked.

She looked at the youngster, eye to eye, and spoke sincerely. "Yes, of course I did, Lyle. It was the neatest one of all of them. I liked the way you had the note so you could read it from the outside. If I'd have made one, I would have copied your idea. But don't tell the other kids I said yours was the nicest. We wouldn't want them to feel bad, would we?"

He looked up at her, again, and reflected, with all the pre-pubescent wisdom he could muster from within, which wasn't a whole lot, given his age, and lack of experience with any mental dealings regarding the opposite sex. "Wasn't he being just a tad immature, and unrealistic?" he thought. "Wasn't she just a little too old for him. Were there not other girls? Was she not suited more to someone like Mr. Jackson? Hadn't he already displayed enough stupidity for one day?" He had one of those abstract learning moments, which convinced him to suck it up, to act wiser, and to display some development.

"Nope, Miss Davis. I guess not. I wouldn't want *anyone* to feel bad." He subconsciously included himself in that 'anyone'.

His life had progressed beyond Crushville, that most treacherous city on the planet, for daydreaming youth.

Or at least until Miss Nanton, his Grade three teacher, came into his life.

121

Miss Davis Decides

Tom showed up at church on Sunday, looking as though he didn't belong, but there still. He took his spot on the bench at the rear. No pew for this guy.

It had been a strenuous ordeal to drag his butt out of bed, from the smoke hangover. His cousin Roland had brought two five-finger lids (bags) of the green stuff, up from Seattle. On the first night they smoked almost half of the one bag, in celebration, of their reunion, and to start the summer off right, as Roland put it. Tom had been bored and smoke-dry for too long, here on the Canadian prairie, and any resemblance of Seattle culture he was used to was a welcome respite from the mundane ruralness of this place. Although he had tried to culturally adjust, it had been just too far a leap.

Then on Saturday they had more for breakfast, before driving down to the teacherage, which Tom had to be out of by August 15 th, so the new teacher could move in. His request for a transfer from the in-the-middle-of-nowhere school had been granted. He had threatened the local board that he'd resign, and teachers were hard to come by, so his request had been granted. He at least got to go to a small town, on a major highway.

On the way down from the city, he had explained to Roland. "There's only one more thing I have to do here."

Roland, until then, had thought that his cousin's job here, in the very-rural spot, was completely over. Apparently not. "What's that?" he inquired.

"There's a young good-looking student minister down the road at the church. She's from Edmonton. Before I leave, I have to seduce her."

Roland laughed. "Yeah, right. You always think you're so good at that. Back in Seattle, back on those beaches, the only reason you were successful was that the girls there wanted it too. You were no seducer. You just happened to be in the right place at the right time. Besides, we were all so stoned half the time no one ever cared. Heck, the girls probably hardly noticed how ugly you are."

Tom went on to explain further. "Well, that may be, but I had her down by a river a couple of weeks ago, and got her to go skinny-dipping with me. Heck of a start, wouldn't you say?"

Indeed, it was. Roland's tune changed. He knew Tom wouldn't be lying. "Well, then maybe you've lucked on to one that needs to rebel. If that's the case, I guess I'm happy for you. Is she pretty?"

Tom smiled, knowing he was one up on Cousin. "Ha. She's incredible. You should have seen her in the river. She would make those girls in Seattle we hung out with look like wrinkled old women."

"Well, then, best of luck in your conquest, Old Boy."

"You can meet her tomorrow, if you come to church with me." Tom knew that sounded odd.

Roland figured Cousin Tom had never been to church in his life, until now. "Are you kidding? Me in church? No way. You go ahead. By the sounds of things, *she's seducing you.* Pretty soon you're gonna have to quit smoking and drinking. You'll be a changed man. For the worse. I'll stay here and wander around your school, or something."

After church, Tom approached the seducee. "So how did the kid party at the river go? I'm sorry I couldn't drive. But I picked up my cousin from Edmonton."

Her face lit up. "Oh, we managed without you. Two of the mothers drove, and the kids had a lot of fun. They find that river interesting, too. We put a lot of bottles into the river to float away. That part was pretty dreamy. Even I had a fine time imagining the possibilities."

"So when are you headed back?"

"Tonight there is a dinner for me at the Sampson's and Mrs. Sampson is going over my report with me. I'm a bit nervous about it. Then I have a couple of days. I'm going back to the city on Wednesday."

This community was something Tom understood well. If they hadn't complained about him, they for sure wouldn't about her. "Don't worry at all. These people are not the criticising type. You've been great. They all listen at the sermons. Everyone seems to really admire you. Especially the little kids."

She laughed. "That's another story. I'll tell you some time."

Tom realised other folks were standing around hoping to have congratulatory or goodwill words with her, before she departed the community. This was her last Sunday sermon. He made his invitation quick. "So can we get together before you go? You know, exchange addresses, and the like. Maybe we could go to the river for a picnic or something."

"That sounds like fun. I'm really busy this afternoon. How about tomorrow?"

"I'll pick you up about noon, then." Tom's eyes looked somewhat clearer now, not quite as red as at the beginning of the day. He wandered off to his VW, a satisfied grin on his face. There actually were valid reasons for attending church. Just that one person's valid reason would have been another's horror.

"Don't bring lunch. I will," she offered.

He agreed, happily. His fridge was nigh empty, from the marijuana munchies he and Roland had gotten into.

Back at the teacherage, Roland welcomed his cousin with a joint. It was obvious Roland had been indulging already. "So did you arrange already for this great seduction, or did you get it on with her right there in church?"

"Nope. Not right there. Although that may have raised a few eyebrows to be sure. I'm taking her to the river tomorrow for a picnic."

"Oh goody. Can I come?" Marijuana had turned Roland into a simplistic goofy sort, momentarily.

Tom laughed. "Definitely not."

Roland put on a sarcastic mocking baby face. "But you said you were going to show me a good time."

"You'll have a good time all by yourself, just as long as that packet of stuff doesn't run out. By the way, I thought you were bringing some for me."

"I did. This is your bag I'm smoking."

Tom shook his head. "Nothing ever changes with you, Buddy, does it? Ever since I've known you."

"Oh don't worry. I hid some more in my bags somewhere. If you don't come back with me, I'll leave you a little. It's about time you went to Edmonton, and found a dealer. That place seemed big enough to me."

"From what I've seen Canadians haven't even heard of this stuff." The culture shock had made Tom somewhat cynical. He had forgotten that the Canada he had seen was only one small rural area of Alberta. It was no Montreal, or Vancouver.

Tom awoke Monday, stupored even more than on Sunday, from the cumulative effect of the drug. When Roland offered him the 'breakfast' toke, he declined, remembering that this was to be the day of the illustrious seduction.

"Oh, just have a little toke," Roland said. "You'll be right over it by noon."

Tom understood himself, and the habit better than that. If he took one, he'd take another, and this seducing duty of his would be one of those grand schemes that never come to pass because of the apathy brought on by marijuana. "Nope." He remained firm throughout the morning, and even walked outside to fresh air to avoid the second hand stuff, just in case, each time Cousin lit up.

At eleven, he went for a bath, a shave, and a spruce-up. He would have to be at his very finest in all ways. Looking in the mirror, he wished he didn't have such bloodshot eyes, but he could always explain that away, as being 'too much driving' as he had in the past.

Cousin called to him as he marched determinedly to the Volks. "Have fun, now!" Drugged Roland wasn't even sure what Tom was up to, but he did remember it had something to do with 'fun'.

Gladys had been doing a whole lot of reflecting, in the evenings, especially, before retiring, at night. She would hold her Bible on her lap, close her eyes, and meditate on all her recent experiences. Still she was unsure of this path she was on. The skinny-dipping episode with this fun-loving fellow from the States certainly was different, if not completely attractive. She still wished she had more time, but that was not the case. Would this be a chance at love, lost, because she could not decide?

Working with the children, and the community had pulled her the other way, to a ministry, that could be hers for the taking, should she decide. Mrs. Sampson had given her a totally glowing report, regarding the whole gamut of ministering, including inspiring sermons, a gift for communication, and the ability to organise, and manage children. It was just the kind of report she needed to continue her ministry. Surely she would be desired anywhere in Western Canada, and there were lots of openings for full time clerics. She was single, and could therefore work for less salary. Opportunities were endless, especially if you included overseas missionary work as an option.

Such is the case with church work. Do you follow your heart or your instincts? The episode with Tom had, for the first time in her life, opened up other possibilities: marriage, love, settling down to have a family, and kids. To do that with a well respected schoolteacher was even more appealing. His was a job of service too. Perhaps she could even continue on somewhere, more towards lay ministry, the way Mrs. Sampson or her own Mother did.

Then there was the man-woman sexuality thing. That was also part of this choice. The skinny-dipping had created new thoughts and flows she didn't even know she had. Was it love, or was it lust? She didn't know. Whichever the case, the feelings were engaging ones. She liked Tom, as a man, and she knew the feelings were mutual. Then again, was he really the man for her? She didn't know him very well at all. Maybe he was even better than she thought. He hadn't tried anything beyond getting her to skinny-dip that day. That was admirable. Even charming. And he seemed legitimately concerned about her, and her problems with the decisions.

She hoped that the outing on Monday would help bring some resolution to all this internal conflict.

Tom was glad it was Monday. That meant there was little likelihood of anybody else being along the river. Sunday was the day for recreational drives here, and Monday was the day all the farmers got back to work. If he was going to seduce this girl in the great outdoors, this was his chance. He felt pretty optimistic on the drive to her place, momentarily the Sampson's. All the members of the community, who volunteered, boarded out the student ministers in three-day shifts, and Mrs. Sampson had purposefully scheduled herself as the last one. Gladys had moved in Sunday night, to the joy of Becky and Anne.

The Volkswagen pulled up just about noon. The girls watched as Gladys climbed in to the passenger seat. They had helped her pack the lunch, somewhat nervously. They were certainly not going bicycling by any rivers today. Mrs. Sampson asked them, "So, Girls, do you think they might be a couple some day?"

Becky answered, "It's hard to tell, Mom. I mean, they're both moving away. They would have to keep in touch by mail, or something."

Marie Sampson's eyes went dreamy, remembering her own romance, how she had overcome a similar distance. "Yes, but love goes a long way. People will make big adjustments."

"Only time will tell, Mom. Don't get your hopes up." Becky spoke wisely, for her age.

Tom figured the best spot would be the famed skinny-dipping place. It would bring back some pleasant memories for both of them. Maybe they could start about where they'd left off.

"Somehow I figured this would be where you'd be going." She smiled at her prediction."But you're not planning on swimming today, are you?"

"No, I'm not. Last time was fun enough. Besides, I already proved I could walk across the river." He didn't lie, about not planning to swim. For he had other, more advanced plans, this time.

Gladys was relieved. "That's good. I sort of got caught up in the moment last time. It was fun and all, but I think if someone would have seen us, it would have been trouble for me, especially. Besides, I want to talk about us."

This he didn't want to hear. This meant she was thinking seriously about him. Perhaps it was useful for immediate gratification, if he lied, but he sure wasn't ready to commit to anything. "Okay. I agree."

The spot looked the same as it had two weeks earlier, and she found a space closer to the road, before the bushes and path to the river. She put down a blanket, and spread out the food. "Well, here it is. I hope you enjoy it. The girls enjoyed helping me pack it."

"Looks good." He sat down cross-legged on one side.

She did likewise, making sure to fold her skirt properly as she sat. She started right in, on her topic. "So do you see us going anywhere? I mean, I like you, and all, and we're both moving. It's all pretty confusing. Have you been thinking about it at all?"

Tom was too busy eating, and plotting how he could change this into his grand seduction, to be listening well. "Yeah. I've been thinking about it a bit."

"So what do you think, then"? she asked.

He avoided the topic. "I think today will be a relaxing day, and one we'll both remember. I often don't really think too far into the future. Whatever happens happens, you know."

"Well, yes. I know that. But still, don't you think it's good to think ahead a bit? Even you have plans for next year, where you're going to be, and that."

"You're right. I do have plans. But I also think that life has to have spontaneity. You enjoyed swimming in the river, didn't you? We never planned that. Yet it was still a whole lot of fun."

Gladys was gong to get this guy narrowed down, or else. "You *might* have planned it all along. How do I know? But you're right that I didn't plan it."

Lunch, being almost complete, allowed him to change the topic. "Let's just go for a walk along the river, there. I want to relax with you. I don't want to get into long drawn out conversations just yet. There will be lots of time for that."

She agreed, but inside it was reluctantly. "Okay." She stood up, and stretched, looking over in the direction of the river.

He stood, too, walked over, and grabbed her hand, and started hiking with her down the footpath. "I wonder what interesting sights we might see over there today." He pointed in the direction of the river.

When they arrived, she headed straight back to the rock she had sat on, in meditation, the other time. There was a comfort in the familiarity. He stood behind her, and put his hands on her shoulders, and started to massage them, in the guise of easing tension in her neck and shoulders.

She stared at the water gently flowing by, and started dreamily philosophising. "I think rivers have ways of imparting knowledge, if one is willing to wait, and reflect. There is something soothing here. Can you feel it?"

"Yes, I can feel it," he uttered. What he was feeling was not what she was feeling. Still they each had strong thoughts.

Her thoughts about the river were legitimate. It did have its way of imparting knowledge. The Godsend she had been wishing for arrived. Finally.

Two things happened simultaneously, each offering up strong spiritual clues on its own, but in combination the impact was staggering, especially for her, as she had been brought up with strong faith, and a belief in signs. Firstly, she saw a bottle with a note in it floating by. She recognised it as Lyle's. She was overwhelmed with the mystic power of his innocence, when she thought of him. It was pure, simple, majestic, and overpowering.

At the same time, his hands gently moved beyond her shoulders to the front of her blouse, and began reaching downwards, towards her breasts.

She stood, moved by the timing. Lyle, or God, or perhaps her own conscience had rescued her. The reason mattered not. The fact remained. She was saved from committing a possible life-lasting mistake.

"You can take me home now!" she declared, triumphantly, and decisively. There was not even a minuscule twinge of doubt in her tone.

He understood, completely. He wasn't all that dumb. The force of her statement was so strong, so compelling, that he had no choice but to understand.

He heaved a heavy sigh. He'd lost. Cousin Roland and his bags of self-indulgent pleasure-making weed would have to do, for now.

Other Books by This Author

<u>Battle On!</u> published 1997 ISBN 0-9683020-0-9

Ordering from Wilson Freelance

To order any books from Wilson Freelance, simply write a note stating the number and the titles. Enclose a cheque or money order payable to Wilson Freelance, for the total + 7% GST + 10% shipping and handling. US orders ignore the GST. (Booksellers should contact the publisher, Wilson Freelance, for wholesale discount prices)

Prices
- Battle On! $13.99 Canadian, 10.99 US
- How Goes the Battle? $13.99 Canadian, 10.99 US

Website address - http://www.compusmart.ab.ca/wilfree/index.html
Email address - mail to:wilfree@compusmart.ab.ca
Fax - 1-403-463-2751
Mailing Address - 1039-73St. Edmonton, AB Canada T6K 3K7

For each book sold, Wilson Freelance donates $1 towards Alzheimer's research.